Praise for

"Archer captures the voices and vulnerabilities of her characters with precision."
—*Publishers Weekly* on *Sandwiched*

"A deeply emotional story of one woman's journey toward forgiveness. A tender tale of life's choices and the joys and sorrows they bring. *The Me I Used To Be* will warm your heart and lift your spirit. A must-read for women of all ages!"
—Ronda Thompson, *New York Times* bestselling author of *The Wild Wulfs of London* series

"Brilliantly conceived and written by Jennifer Archer, *The Me I Used To Be* is a poignant tale of one woman's road to self-discovery. What she learns along the way is so touchingly emotional you can't put the book down."
—Candace Havens, author of *Charmed and Dangerous*

"Jennifer Archer's *The Me I Used To Be* is a luminous novel, rich with depth, humor and unforgettable characters. A poignant tale of long-lost loves and the redemptive promise of tomorrow, *The Me I Used To Be* is a standout in quality women's fiction. Look for more from this talented author; Jennifer Archer is one to watch."
—Britta Coleman, author of *Potter Springs*

Jennifer Archer

As a frequent speaker at writing workshops, women's events and creative writing classes, award-winning author Jennifer Archer enjoys inspiring others to set goals and pursue their dreams. She is the mother of two grown sons and currently resides in Texas with her high school sweetheart and their neurotic Brittany spaniel. Jennifer enjoys hearing from her readers through her Web site www.jenniferarcher.net.

JENNIFER ARCHER

my perfectly imperfect life

MY PERFECTLY IMPERFECT LIFE

copyright © 2006 by Jennifer Archer

isbn 0373880847

This edition published by arrangement with Harlequin Books S.A.

® and TM are trademarks of the publisher. Trademarks indicated with
® are registered in the United States Patent and Trademark Office, the
Canadian Trade Marks Office and in other countries.

TheNextNovel.com

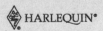 HARLEQUIN®

PRINTED IN U.S.A.

From the Author

Dear Reader,

I have four siblings. One older than I, and three younger. In a lot of ways, we have very little in common other than our parents and pieces of our pasts. We don't look that much alike, we don't work in the same fields, we have many different interests and hobbies. Still, thankfully, we have never had the sort of turbulent relationship that Dinah and Dottie Dewberry, the sisters in this book, share. Though we've had our conflicts, my siblings and I are close and have never suffered a rift that has kept us apart for years, or even months.

Once, during a conversation with one of my sisters, she posed a question that has intrigued me ever since. If we weren't related and we had met, would we have ended up friends? We decided we would have. But, considering our different personalities, was that just hopeful thinking?

I wrote *My Perfectly Imperfect Life* to examine the relationship of two sisters and what happens when their trust in one another is shattered. I wanted to explore the effects betrayal, resentment and shame can have on a family bond that was once tied tight with love and understanding. Dinah and Dottie continually surprised me. The unusual circumstances they find themselves caught up in as reluctant allies made me laugh one minute and cry the next. I hope their story will surprise and touch you, too. And make you smile.

Happy reading,

Jennifer Archer

For my mother-in-law, Dorothy Archer,
who loves a good laugh and
a good book.
Thanks for sharing both with me
through the years.

Austin, Texas
Spring, 1989

Dinah

The scent of roses and prime rib filled the candle-lit country club dining room; the smell of my salvation. I had waited my entire life for this night. Not only did I love Blaine, he was my escape route from Coopersville. From my past. He would make me a Medford. A somebody. Part of a decent, respectable family. One day, we would have children. They would hold their heads high and be proud of their name. They would never hesitate to bring friends to our home.

Blaine squeezed my fingers beneath the crisp, white tablecloth. Then, releasing my hand, he tapped his fork against a crystal wineglass, pushed away from the table and stood. Everyone fell silent.

"Mom and Dad…Audra." He shifted his attention from his parents and sister to our small group of guests. "Thanks, everyone, for coming tonight to celebrate my passing the bar exam. Dad, you can finally exhale that breath you've been holding. Good thing, too. You're turning blue."

I drank in the titters of laughter like champagne bubbles; they made me just as giddy. When Blaine turned to me, I stood, too.

"But we have something even better to celebrate." He took my hand. "Last week, I asked Dinah to marry me, and she accepted."

The room erupted with words of congratulations from our friends, but the Medfords' silence rolled over me like a boulder, squashing my happiness.

Paige Medford's thin smile never wavered as she exchanged a glance with her daughter that told me more than words ever could.

Blaine's father cleared his throat, his eye twitching above a forced grin. "That's wonderful, Son. We're so pleased, Dinah."

Dropping my hand and frowning, Blaine said, "Mother?"

Mrs. Medford glanced from him, to our silent

guests, to me. "We *are* pleased. Just taken off guard. Shouldn't your family be here for this occasion? Your sister? Your aunt? We've never even met them."

The first time I visited Blaine's family, I said my parents were dead, that I wasn't close to my sister or my aunt. All true. My mother and father might have been living and breathing somewhere on the planet but, to me, they *were* dead and had been for fifteen years. And since leaving home for college at the age of eighteen, I rarely saw Aunt Maeve or Dottie. "They couldn't come," I said quickly. "My aunt isn't well."

"I'm so sorry to hear that." The flickering candles on the table failed to soften Mrs. Medford's stare. "And where did you tell me they live?"

"Coopersville. It's a small town north of Amarillo."

"And your sister?"

"She has finals. She's at Texas Tech finishing her sophomore year."

Which wasn't true, at all. My younger sister had never set foot in a college classroom.

Eyes bored into me. The judgmental eyes of Blaine's family. The pitying eyes of our friends. Why wouldn't Blaine say anything? He watched his parents closely, his face taut and worried, the sparkle of excitement he had worn all evening extinguished.

Mr. Medford raised his wineglass. "This calls for a toast."

I reached for my glass but stopped short of lifting it when a commotion sounded beyond the doorway.

"Miss!" the waiter called out. "You can't go in there. It's a private party."

"Get your hands off me! I can do whatever the hell I want. I'm about to be a part of this snooty family."

The familiar slurred smoke-and-velvet voice shot my heart toward the ceiling then dropped it to the floor. Turning, I stepped away from the table. Gasps and whispers drifted from behind me. The room swayed. The chandelier's lights blurred. The draperies bled crimson. Every sound seemed too loud, distorted.

One step ahead of the frantic waiter, Dottie burst into the room wearing a tube top, short flared skirt, fishnet tights cut off at midcalf, and more beads and bangles than Madonna. Shoulder-length, overbleached and permed hair formed a wild halo around her face. She took in the scene with bleary, mascara-coated eyes, her full cherry-red lips pursed, as if for a kiss.

Planting one hand on an out-thrust hip, Dottie tilted her head and sneered, "Well, well, well. Look at Aunt Maeve's little lemon drop now. You did good for yourself, Dinah. This is quite a step up from the trailer park. Just what you've always wanted." She moved nearer to me on unsteady legs, and I almost gagged on the fog of alcohol and tobacco fumes surrounding her.

"Dottie, please…"

Pausing in front of Blaine, Dottie sized him up: his styled sandy hair, the conservative tie, the dark suit, the polished, tasseled shoes. She fanned her face. "Nice, Dinah. So this must be my future brother-in-law." Linking her arm through his, she pressed closer to Blaine's side, pecked his cheek, purred, "Welcome to the family, good-lookin'."

Blaine flinched. The red imprint of Dottie's lips stained the space beside his mouth. Glaring at me, he breathed, "*Do* something about her, or *I* will."

"Why are you here?" I hissed, grabbing her arm.

"Hey! Back off." Dottie laughed and jerked away. "You don't think I'd miss my big sister's engagement party, do you?"

"You weren't invited."

"That's right, I wasn't." The tone of her voice hardened along with her eyes. "Neither was Aunt Maeve. You didn't even *tell* her. Why not just slap her in the face? That's what it felt like when she heard your big news from the mailman."

Kay's father. I should have never confided in my

best friend from back home. I glanced over my shoulder at Blaine's humiliated eyes. Behind him, his family and friends stared at Dottie, their faces masks of disgust.

"You think you're better than us." Dottie dug the spiked heels of her ankle boots into the thick carpet as I tried to drag her toward the door. "You've always thought so. But you're not." She looked back at the table and yelled, "She's not. She's plain old Dinah Dewberry from Ponderosa Mobile Home Park in Coopersville. No college degree or rich husband's gonna change that."

Vibrating with humiliation and rage, I shoved my sister into the hallway and stepped out beside her.

Dottie fell back against the wall, her bravado crumbling. With a sob, she clutched her stomach and lifted hazy eyes to mine. "I'm sorry, Di...I—"

"No." Shaking my head, I raised a hand to stop Dottie's words. "I won't accept your apology. Not this time."

"I'm gonna be sick. I need you."

"You need me too much. You always have. I'm through taking care of you, do you understand? I'm through covering for you and bailing you out of trouble every time you screw up. I don't care what happens to you anymore. As far as I'm concerned, we're not sisters."

Dottie swiped at her eyes with a trembling hand, smearing mascara across her cheek. "You stopped being my sister a long time ago," she whispered. Pushing away from the wall, she stumbled down the hallway past the waiter and a staring string of the country club's staff.

Choking on tears, I turned and walked in the opposite direction. When I reached the emergency exit, I shoved through it, tripping an alarm.

I didn't look back.

CHAPTER 1

Amarillo, Texas
Summer 2006

Dinah

June in the landlocked Texas Panhandle feels like a sauna. Dry heat. Not a drop of water in sight to cool off in. No ocean. No raging river. No babbling brook. I'm the only one doing those things. Brooding, raging and babbling, that is. I sit in my backyard at the patio table wearing only my slip. My old black Labrador retriever, Saxon, lies at my feet, panting steadily.

"I guess we better go back inside to the air-conditioning," I murmur to him. "My makeup is melting."

When I glance at his grizzled face, Saxon's tail thumps the patio's concrete floor.

"Just one more minute." I listen for the sound of Stan's truck in the alley. We're the only house on the block with a rear-entry garage.

Saxon whines.

"He'll be here."

The dog whines again, and I swear I see pity in his eyes.

"He'll *be* here," I repeat, but I can't blame him for doubting. Saxon has been through too many other nights with me that started out like this one. The two of us alone. Waiting in the darkness for Stan to come home from his job as a cop. He always shows up. Sometimes later than others. During those minutes or hours, or even days, when he should be home but isn't, I feel as though I'm holding my breath, and the same old worries bombard me. Is he in danger? Hurt again?

Then Stan walks through the door in one piece, and I exhale.

That's what will happen tonight, I assure myself. He couldn't get away from work, that's all. But it's my birthday, for crying out loud. Forty years. Can't he at least be on time this once? Not that I really feel like celebrating, but we have reservations at Piper's. Stan knows that; it was his idea. But that was this morning. Who knows what's gone on in his life since then? Not me, that's for damn sure.

I take deep breaths to steady my nerves. Now I understand why the woman Stan almost married, years before we met, broke off their engagement. He said she was unreasonable about his work. Unreasonable? She probably couldn't handle all the worry and loneliness, and I don't blame her. If I could've seen into the future and known the reality of being a cop's wife, maybe I would have backed out of the marriage, too.

Laughter drifts from the house across the alley, and I hear a baby's delighted squeal. Despair wraps strong arms around me and squeezes, bringing tears to my eyes. The home pregnancy test was negative again this morning. Oh, I figured it would be, but it still hurts to see the evidence of another failure. Each time my period is even a day late, I tell myself not to get excited, not to expect anything. But an ember of hope still smolders somewhere deep inside me. It flickers a bit then flares as one late day turns into another, then another until, finally, I perform the same ritual that I've perfected over the past five years.

These are the instructions the manufacturer *should* have written on the box: *Pee on the strip, watch the clock for five minutes, hold your breath and pace. Pray, if you're so inclined.*

I won't tell Stan. Facing him with the bad news gets harder each time. I want to enjoy dinner and put it out of my mind. Or try to. I'm the one with the problem, not him. Endometriosis. Started when I was thirty. Before that, I probably could have gotten pregnant without any difficulty, or so the doctors tell me. But I didn't meet Stan until I was thirty-four, and we didn't marry until the next year.

We'll just have to try again, like always. Maybe I'll even follow Aunt Maeve's advice and buy a yellow pair of booties, tuck them away in a safe place. She swears that's the key to conception.

Forty. No big deal. Lots of women my age have babies these days. Even so, I admit I'm starting to panic. It feels as if the time allotted for me to conceive is slipping away, the sand falling faster through the hourglass, picking up the pace with each grain that sifts through.

Stan's truck rumbles at the end of the alley, pulling me from my thoughts. "Told you so," I say to Saxon, then nudge him with my toe.

A cool rush of air hits my face when I open the French doors leading from the patio into our bedroom. Saxon limps along beside me toward the closet. I hear the door from the garage into the kitchen open then shut.

"Dinah?" Stan calls out.

"In here."

Saxon limps toward the door at the sound of Stan's voice.

I search the closet for my black dress, expecting my husband to appear at any moment. But when the door to our home office down the hall squeaks, I know Stan must be checking his e-mail.

I shove one hanger across the rod, then another. He can't even say hello first. His job, that damn e-mail, or whatever it is he looks at on the computer lately, takes precedence over everything. Even our efforts to conceive.

Just yesterday morning, at four to be precise, I walked up behind him where he sat at our home computer. He almost shot through the ceiling when I spoke his name. Thanks to his quick punch of a button, the screen went black before I could glimpse what he studied with such focused intensity. There have been other nights, too, when I've awoken to find the bed empty and the computer monitor's glow illuminating the shadowed hallway.

Lifting the dress from the hanging rod, I step from the closet and drape it over a chair in the corner, then reach for the zipper.

Stan radiates tension when he walks into the room a second later. That's nothing new. But tonight there's an edge to it that alerts all my senses. I glance across at him and force a smile. "Hi, sweetie." *You're late.*

He rolls his left shoulder and winces, stretches his head from side to side.

"Your neck bothering you?"

"Yeah. It's stiff."

Probably from all the late nights he spends on the computer. "I'll give you a massage later. Why don't you make us a drink while I finish getting ready?"

After another left-to-right neck stretch and a glance at me, he starts to leave, then does a double take, his focus on my slip. "Don't change a thing." His mouth turns up at one corner. "You look good just like that." He leans against the door frame, his jacket slung over his shoulder. As he reaches to pat Saxon's head, his gaze moves slowly down my body.

Since we're already late, I don't want to encourage what his expression tells me he has in mind. "My usual martini," I say. "Extra dirty, no—"

"—Vermouth, four olives and a twist of lemon," he finishes for me.

I lower the zipper on my dress then glance up to see that he hasn't moved. Tiny strands of silver streak his tousled dark brown hair. His sun-bronzed face, with its wide mouth, narrow nose and cleft chin, is lined by life, adding a touch of ruggedness to his appearance that suits him. Even after five years of marriage, the sight of him still stirs awareness in me. The slow, casual way he moves, his broad shoulders and narrow hips, the desire in his eyes at certain times when we're together; times like now. All of it has the power to steal my breath, to make me forget my irritation.

Stan leaves Saxon and walks toward me, placing his jacket on the chair. He unbuckles his belt and tugs his shirttail free of his waistband. The directness of his gaze unnerves me as I raise the dress to slip it over my head.

"Wait," he says.

I lower my arms.

"Don't put that on." He nods me over. "Come here."

"I thought your neck was stiff?" I tease.

He grins. "So is something else."

I'm not sure why my heart races as I smile and step toward him. Something about him seems dangerous tonight. An exciting sort of danger, not one I fear.

"You're in a strange mood," I say, tilting my head.

He takes the dress from my hands, tosses it on the chair beside his jacket.

"It'll get wrinkled."

"I don't want you to wear it, anyway." Stan trails a fingertip from my elbow to my shoulder.

"But it's your favorite dress."

"I like this better." He lowers one strap on my slip, skimming my shoulder with his palm, scattering goose bumps over my skin.

I laugh again. "I can't wear this to Piper's."

Confusion flickers in his eyes, but he quickly covers it.

"You forgot, didn't you?" Frustrated all over again, I back up, lifting my slip strap into place.

"I didn't forget." Moving closer, Stan lowers the opposite strap. "It's your birthday. I just had a better idea how we might celebrate it."

"I thought you wanted to go out?"

He pulls me to him. "That was before I saw you in this."

I want to stop him when his palm covers my breast, to tell him that tonight I'm going to have things my way, not his. We're going to Piper's. Case closed. But because work has kept him so busy, too much time has passed since he touched me like this. The heat and pressure of his hand feels too good, too right. "We have reservations for eight o'clock," I protest weakly.

His mouth meets the curve of my neck, the brush of his lips starting an ache at my center. "The only thing I want to eat right now," he murmurs, "is you."

I kiss him back when his lips touch mine. God, he tastes good. Like—I pull back slightly. "Have you been eating strawberries?"

Stan's head jerks up, his startled eyes meet mine.

"What? No...I—" He lifts me into his arms so suddenly I gasp.

"We can be late," I murmur. "I've missed you."

"I've missed you, too."

I stroke a finger across the beard stubble on his chin. "As soon as your new business with Pete gets going we'll have plenty of opportunities for more nights at home like this. More chances to make a baby."

A muscle at the edge of Stan's jawline jumps. He puts me down, glances away.

"Stan?"

He starts around the bed, as if needing it between us before he can speak.

Saxon whimpers and lifts his head off the floor.

"What's wrong?"

"I decided not to go into partnership with Pete."

"But, why? Not two weeks ago you were talking about—" I pull up my strap. "It's this new case you're working, isn't it?"

"The case is only part of it. I'm a cop, Dinah, not a pencil pusher. I'd go crazy sitting behind a desk. Even if I owned it."

"I thought you were excited about starting a security business?"

"I tried to be. I know how much it means to you. You've been on edge ever since Pete's accident."

A familiar fear shudders through me at the thought of Pete Conrad, once so vital and strong, now confined to a wheelchair.

"I was afraid if I didn't quit…"

He doesn't need to finish the statement. He was afraid we wouldn't last. I know that without hearing him say the words. His ex-partner's shooting only added to the stress between us. Stress over his job, the long hours and dangerous situations he faces on a daily basis. Stress over the guest room down the hallway that should be a nursery by now. Our marriage already stood on shaky ground before Pete's tragedy. I'd be naive to think Stan hadn't noticed the same cracks in the foundation that I did.

Crossing the room, I grab my dress off the chair, clutch it to my chest and meet his gaze. "How are we supposed to raise a family with you gone so much? And what if something happened to you? I don't want to be a single parent, Stan."

"I saw the strip in the wastebasket this morning, Dinah. Don't you think it's time we—" He looks away.

"What? Give up? The doctors say—"

"They've been saying that for five years. We've tried almost everything."

"*Almost.* There are other procedures we could look into."

"This is starting to take over our lives. You're consumed with it."

"It's important to me." I turn away from him.

"It is to me, too. But having a baby isn't everything." He walks over and pulls me around to face him. "Even when I am home, you're always so moody and down. Sure, I'd like to have kids, but it's not a requirement for me to be happy."

"Well, it is for me. You told me you were willing to go the distance."

"I didn't know it would take so much. Especially from you. Every month, you drop into a black hole."

"Not this time. I was handling it." His change of heart hurts. I need him on my side in this. All I've ever wanted was to give a child the family life I never had. Two loving parents, a nice house, a stable home. How can I give that up? "You used to want a family as much as I do."

"We're older now. I'm ready to move on."

"Maybe you just don't want a baby with *me*. Is that it?" I toss the dress to the floor. My bruised heart is talking for me now; I don't really believe what I'm saying.

Stan steps back and throws up his hands. "Don't turn this into something else."

"It would explain why you're putting in even longer

hours now. Why you've been acting so jumpy and shutting me out."

Not that he hasn't before on occasion, but this time is worse, different somehow. Again, I remember finding him at the computer, the way he flinched and cleared the screen when I said his name.

"I'm caught up in this case, that's all. If you can't trust me—"

"Are you sure it's the *case* that has you so tied up in knots?"

Stan's eyes narrow. "What else would tie me up in knots, Dinah? Are you implying that I'm cheating on you?"

"Are you?"

"You know me better than that. I'd never betray our marriage."

I do know him. But why do I sense that something isn't right?

Crossing to the bed, I tug and smooth the rumpled linens. "I feel like I spend all my time waiting. Waiting for you to come home. Waiting for you to share what's going on in your life." My voice cracks as I reach for the blanket and say quietly, "Waiting for a baby."

Maybe that's my fate in life. When I was young, I waited, too. For my mother to call. For my father to come back for Dottie and me. And, later, to escape Coopersville and my family's reputation.

"I hate being alone so much," I whisper. What I don't tell him, is that it makes me feel deserted all over again.

"I'm a detective. You knew that when you married me. If you can't deal with it…"

We don't have any business being together.

His unspoken words hang heavy between us. I pick up a pillow, crush it against my middle, wrap my arms around it.

"So…" Stan exhales noisily.

We stare at each other across a long stretch of silence. "I feel like you're shutting me out."

"What do you want me to say?" When I don't respond, he adds, "Are you bailing on me?"

How can he ask that? He knows my history; I'm the one always left behind. What I see in his expression startles me. He thinks I'm no different than the people who betrayed me. That I run away from problems rather than facing them, like my mother and father did. And maybe he's right. I ran from Coopersville. From Dottie and Aunt Maeve. From my engagement to Blaine.

"I'm not bailing out on you. But when I did that pregnancy test this morning and saw the results, I felt like I couldn't even turn to you, like you wouldn't have time for me or wouldn't want to listen. You're walking on eggshells lately, but you don't trust me enough to tell me what's wrong."

"*I* don't trust *you?*" Stan utters a sound of disbelief. "It's always all about you, isn't it? About what *you* want."

I lay the pillow on the bed and jab a finger against my chest. "I take care of me. I always have and I always will. If that's wrong, then count me guilty."

"Fine. Take care of you and forget about us." Muttering under his breath, Stan leaves the bedroom.

Seconds later, when the door to the garage slams, Saxon looks at me and whimpers. I kick the bedpost then, cursing, sit down and rub my toe. *Fine*, he said. Well it's fine with me, too. Forget Piper's. Forget my birthday. Forget this marriage. I'm through.

I let the tears fall, laughing through my misery when Saxon licks them off my knees. "Enough of this," I say with a sniff, scratching his head. I'm only fooling myself. I won't leave Stan. I can't. I love him too much. And he's wrong about me. I don't bail out when things get tough. Not anymore. I'm stronger than that now. I'm not like my parents.

As I go to pick up the dress I dropped on the floor, I wonder how I can fix the trouble between us. *Am I* being unreasonable, wanting Stan to quit the force? I could have told anyone five minutes after meeting him that the man isn't made to run a business or work in an office. He'd feel like a caged animal in no time flat. He's a cop through and through.

I reach for my dress, then notice Stan's jacket on the chair above it. Something hangs from the pocket. Something thin and narrow, dark and shiny. A strap. A premonition that my world is about to shift overwhelms me and, for a second, I wonder if Aunt Maeve's superstitious nature has finally rubbed off on me. Hooking my finger through the strap I pull it free.

My breath catches.

It's black. Lacy. A size 42 double D.

I wear a B cup. Barely.

Blinking, I carry the garment closer to the lamp-light for a better inspection. An exotic, spicy, drug-store scent that reminds me again of Aunt Maeve wafts up to tickle my nose. *Stan bought me lingerie for my birthday*, I assure myself, desperate to believe it. *He screwed up on the size, that's all.*

But I know that's ridiculous.

Stan isn't the sort of husband who buys his wife lingerie. And even if he did, a bra this size is no accident. I could put both of my boobs in one of the cups and still have plenty of room left over for a couple of throw pillows.

Clutching the big black bra in my fist, I walk to the bed, sit down and close my eyes. Saxon lays his head in my lap. A minute passes, then two. "How could he?" I whisper. "How could he?"

I dig my fingers into a lacy cup. All the things he said… He wouldn't betray our marriage. I should know him better than to think he'd cheat. Lies. All of them. He looked into my eyes and lied without so much as a blink.

Maybe I should go after him. Have a tantrum. Throw the evidence in his face. Maybe I should pack my bags, take Saxon and disappear for good.

But none of those options seem like enough to soothe my wounded pride. Nothing short of stringing Stan up the nearest flagpole with the big black bra would do that. And even then, I doubt I'd be satisfied.

When the phone rings, I jump and grab the receiver off the nightstand. "Hello?" It's all I can do to squeeze the single word from my swollen throat.

"Is this the Hager residence?"

It's a female voice. Smoky and seductive.

Visions of the other woman play through my mind

like a slide show. An Amazon…a busty bimbo…a lusty
Lolita with luscious curves and come-hither eyes.

Would *she* have the nerve to call him *here*?

I squeeze the receiver tighter. "Who is this?"

CHAPTER 2

"Who is this?" I repeat when the caller doesn't answer me the first time.

"Dinah?"

That voice. I know it.

"This is Dottie."

My stomach turns over. Either I'm having a nightmare, or someone is playing a really bad joke.

"Well? Say something."

No joke. I'd recognize that sassy tone anywhere. I'm not sure who I'd rather talk to least. My long-lost sister, or Stan's other woman. "What's wrong? Is Aunt Maeve okay?"

"Aunt Maeve is fine. I talked to her less than an hour ago, as a matter of fact."

I blink at the bra on the bed beside me and run a finger across the lace. After seventeen years of silence, Dottie had to go and choose today of all days to call. Another failed pregnancy test. Stan's announcement that he isn't quitting the force. Our fight. Finding another woman's underwear in his pocket. Now, this. *Happy birthday*. I don't know how much more fun I can take.

Dottie clears her throat. "It's been a long time. I— um—realized it was your birthday and I thought…" She blurts a laugh. "So how's forty?"

I burst into tears.

"Jesus, calm down. I didn't mean to upset you. I'll hang up."

"No…it isn't you." At least not completely. I wipe my eyes, start to blow my nose, then smell perfume and realize I'm using the bra as a hanky. "You caught me at a bad time, that's all."

"I guess that means I shouldn't drop by, then."

"You're in town?"

"Yeah."

That could only mean more bad news. Why would my sister literally drop back into my life without warning after all this time? Dottie must want something. *Need* something. Obviously, she ran out of doormats, so she's starting over at the beginning of the line with her original doormat. Me. "Are you in trouble?"

"Not exactly. Um, well, sort of. I was hoping we could, you know, talk for a few minutes. Catch up."

"Catch up on seventeen years in a few minutes?" I crumple the bra in my fist. "I don't know, Dottie. Like

I said, it's a bad time. And it's getting late. Why don't we wait until tomorrow? The sun is going down. I don't want you to get lost trying to find your way over here in the dark."

"I won't get lost. I can see your place from here."

"Where are you?"

"Outside."

I push to my feet. "Outside *where?*"

"Your house. In front. Parked at the curb."

I hurry from the bedroom to the living room, push up the slats on the plantation shutters and peek out.

A battered red clunker pulling a U-Haul sits in the street, the left front tire propped up on the curb. The car has a bent bumper, a dented fender, peeling patches of paint. Inside, I glimpse a shadowy, indistinguishable figure.

"Well?" Dottie has the nerve to sound impatient.

Slamming the slats shut, I back away from the window. "What do you expect me to say, Dottie?"

"Come in, would be nice."

Bitterness bubbles up in me. "Fine. Come in."

"Don't break an ankle jumping up and down with excitement."

Saxon limps into the room and meets my gaze, growling low in his throat, as if he senses trouble ahead.

I head for the entry hall. "I'll turn on the porch

light," I tell my sister, half hoping the dog takes a chunk out of her leg and she'll run screaming back to her car.

The second I break the connection, anxiety hits me like a tidal wave. I flip on the outside light, reach for the knob then back away and return to the living room where I pace off my nervous energy in front of the sofa.

When the bell rings, I realize I'm still clutching the bra in my fist. I toss it onto the coffee table and drag myself back to the door. Inhaling deeply, I open it to find a stranger on my porch. *Short wind-tossed henna-red hair. Blunt cheekbones. Too-tan skin. Wrinkles alongside weary, green eyes.* I look deeper into those eyes and finally catch a glimpse of my sister. "Dottie?"

She sets her big leopard-print purse on the floor. "Look at you." I hear a hitch in her voice and, for several more moments, we study each other, mentally chipping away seventeen years of changes, trying to uncover some semblance of a person we remember.

My sister wears faded flared jeans, a low-cut peasant blouse. She's heavier than I've imagined her. The eyelashes are false, as is the penciled-in mole at the side of her mouth. But the pouting lips are the same, stained a deep shade of red.

We both blink, breaking the spell, and Dottie blows in like the wind. After I close the door, I turn to find her beaming at me with a smile that seems hesitant and awkward despite its width. She opens her arms. "Well?"

I manage a smile, too, a shaky one. We hug, and I'm surprised by a rush of love so powerful it weakens my knees. Leaning into my sister, I struggle to hold back the tears that fill my eyes. We end the hug quickly, step back, laugh and hug again. I sense tension in Dottie, that she is as nervous as me over this meeting. Then her shoulders relax and we simply hold each other, something we haven't done since we were kids. And seldom then.

When we finally let go, an uncomfortable silence surrounds us, and we avoid each other's eyes. I clear my throat, call the dog over. "This is Saxon."

Dottie kneels to his level. "Hey, big guy. Aren't you the looker?" She reaches out to him, but Saxon scoots behind me. "Shy, huh? That's okay. You'll warm up to me when you get to know me better."

Does that mean she plans to stay awhile? Now I'm as wary as Saxon, but there's no place for me to hide. I lead Dottie into the living room where we sit side by side on the couch.

She eyes the slip I'm still wearing, since I never dressed after Stan left. "I guess I did catch you at a bad time. I didn't interrupt anything with you and…"

"Stan," I say. "No, he's not home." I'm horrified

when my voice falters and my face screws up. Sobbing, I press two fingers between my brows.

Dottie lifts the black bra from the coffee table. She glances at it then at my chest. Her brow furrows, and she mutters, "That son of a bitch."

I snatch the bra from her hand. "I don't want to talk about it."

"You don't have to be embarrassed with me. I've hooked up with every kind of loser that exists."

"Stan's not a loser."

"Whatever you say."

"He *isn't*." I dissolve into tears again. "It was in his jacket pocket."

Dottie scoots closer, puts an arm around me.

I turn my face into her neck and sob harder. "I don't know why I'm surprised." Wondering where the tissue came from that she stuffs into my hand, I lean back and blow my nose. "The clues were there, I just didn't want to believe what they were telling me."

Her eyes brim with sympathy I never expected.

"Stan's been working a lot of late nights. That's not unusual, really. He's a cop, you know? A detective. But lately his hours are worse than ever. And he's so on edge." I tell her about the computer incident. "We fought tonight."

Before I know it, I'm spilling my guts about Stan's

decision not to quit the force, as well as everything else that's wrong in our marriage. I don't know why. As I recall, confiding in Dottie is a pointless endeavor, but I can't stop myself. I need an ear, a shoulder to cry on. My wayward sister is available. If an encyclopedia salesman had arrived on the doorstep five minutes ago instead of her, my tears would be dripping onto his order forms right now.

Blinking back another onslaught of tears, I lift the bra from my lap and slip my arms through the straps. I stare down at the empty cups. "Look at this." My lower lip quivers. "*Look.*"

Dottie wants to laugh; I see it in her eyes when I glance up. Not at me, or the situation, but at the sight of me wearing the too-big bra over my slip. The thing is, subtract one D from the equation, change the 42 to a 36, and it would fit her. When we were teenagers, she used to tease me about the unpromising state of my chest. I was still waiting to blossom long after she had already been in bloom for quite some time, despite being two years younger than me.

I glare at her, and Dottie puts on a serious face. "Have yourself a good cry." She pats my hand. "Go on, get it out of your system. Then I want you to dry your eyes and take that bra to your husband. The sooner the better."

"And ask him *what?* What does the woman have that I don't?" I poke my finger against one empty bra cup, and the indentation remains after I take away my hand. "I think the answer is pretty obvious."

A giggle slips past her lips. "I'm sorry, Dinah." She covers her mouth with one hand and waves at me with the other. "I'm sorry. Look at it this way, the woman's no super model. I mean, a *42?*" She giggles again.

I take off the bra and keep glaring. Why am I wasting my breath talking to her about this? I don't even know her anymore. Even when I *did* know her, she would've been the last person I turned to with a personal problem.

"Okay." Clearing her throat, she sits straighter and composes herself. "Let's take a deep breath and think this through. Where's your liquor cabinet? What you need is a little Southern Comfort. Then we'll figure this out."

Of course. Since the age of fifteen that's been Dottie's way of dealing with any situation. A few beers or several shots of whiskey straight up. Tie one on. Have a good old time. Everything will work itself out.

"If I start drinking I might never stop," I tell her. "I could use a glass of iced tea, though."

Dottie stands. "I'll make it."

"You don't have to do that. It's already made." I stand, too, and lead her into the kitchen. "Did you just get into town?"

"Yeah."

"You drove all the way from Vegas?"

"It took two days." She pauses in the kitchen with a fist perched on one hip. "You knew I lived in Vegas?"

I take two glasses from the cabinet. "Aunt Maeve fills me in." The truth is, I try to change the subject whenever she brings up Dottie, which is often, but Aunt Maeve just keeps talking. And, honestly, I'm usually curious about what's going on with my sister, though I'd never admit it to her.

Dottie smirks. "She tells me all about you, too. Dinah this and Dinah that. She brags on you until I want to puke. About you being teacher-of-the-year and your good-lookin' husband. I can imagine what she says about me."

"She brags about you, too."

"Oh, yeah, right. What does she say? That I'm about to hit the Guinness Book of World Records for the number of jobs I've lost and the number of men I've laid?"

Actually, Aunt Maeve has kept me up to date on all that. Dottie has become a professional wanderer. From job-to-job, city-to-city, man-to-man. It's as if she's searching for something. Or someone.

I fill the glasses with ice while Dottie fidgets. She slides open my silverware drawer then opens the cabinet where my plates are stacked. Catching her attention, I gesture to the pantry. "The liquor's in there."

"I'll just have tea."

Dottie passing up alcohol? Interesting. More than her looks have changed, I guess.

As I pour the tea, she walks over to the refrigerator and looks at the photos secured on the door by magnets.

"Who are these kids?"

"My last year's kindergarten class."

Her face looks as if she ate a rancid pecan. "I don't understand why you gave up journalism to babysit a bunch of brats."

"They're children, not brats."

"That's only true if they're your own."

I carry the glasses of tea to the table. "I love kids. I enjoy being with them. Besides, I still freelance in the summers. I'm working on a magazine article now."

Studying me, Dottie taps a forefinger against her chin, as if she's either trying to figure me out, or figure out how to ask me something. When I meet her gaze, she glances away quickly, her tongue flicking out to moisten her lips. "Where did I leave my purse?"

"I think you put it down by the door."

"You mind if I smoke?"

"I'd rather you didn't in the house."

"Could we take those drinks outside then?"

"Sure." I start for the backyard, flip on the patio light, call for Saxon. "Find your purse. I'll meet you in back."

"In your slip?"

"Why not? I'm not the prude you always thought I was, Dottie."

Looking amused and doubtful, she leaves the room, and I go outside.

A minute later the back door opens and a scruffy mixed-breed dog half Saxon's size bounds out onto the patio, followed by Dottie. "Meet Hoot Junior," she says, then sits across the table from me and pulls a pack of cigarettes and a lighter from her purse.

"Hoot Junior? Isn't that—?"

"I named him after Aunt Maeve's old mutt, Hoot. Remember him?"

I nod, unable to fathom why she'd want a daily reminder of our childhood. "What was her other dog's name?"

"Holler."

"That's right."

Hoot Junior circles the table twice in a dead run, then pauses to lift his leg on my potted petunias.

"No, Hoot!" Dottie yells. "Get away from those. You have a whole yard to pee in." The dog darts over to sniff Saxon, who lies quietly at my feet looking peeved, and Dottie faces me again. "Sorry. He doesn't know any better. His former owner didn't teach him his p's and q's. He's a sweetie, though. I rescued him from one of my dogsitting clients."

Dogsitting? And she thinks I'm crazy for teaching children?

"He never left Hoot any water when he went to work, and I saw the guy kick him once," she continues. "So the day I left Vegas, I drove over and took him from the backyard."

"You *stole* him?" Now I know I've lost my mind. I've been confiding in my dognapping sister. "Great, Dottie. All I need is for the police to show up at my door to arrest me for harboring a fugitive."

"Don't you have an in with the cops?" Lighting up, she gives me a snide look. "Relax. I'm not holding the dog for ransom. Besides, the jerk's probably thrilled I took Hoot off his hands." She drags deeply on the cigarette, then exhales a stream of smoke that the wind blows toward me.

I wave a hand in front of my face.

"Oh, yeah. I forgot how *sensitive* you are. I'll blow it to the side."

"Thanks," I say, ignoring her sarcasm. When we were teenagers, we fought constantly about her smoking in the bedroom we shared. She didn't believe me when I said I was allergic, that the scent of smoke in my clothing and hair made me sneeze. Dottie always accused me of exaggerating, of being a prim-and-proper prude.

Propping my forearms on the table, I lean forward. "Why are you here, Dottie?"

She takes another long drag. "I lost my job as a cocktail waitress at the casino a couple of weeks back."

So I was right. She's out of work and probably short on cash. She wants money; that's why she came to me. I'm only surprised it took her this long.

"I was late coming in to work three days in a row because I was sick to my stomach. I tried to explain to my boss that I'd drag myself in, sick or not, from then on, but he said it didn't matter. He'd been thinking about letting me go anyway and hiring some young bimbette. Got to keep up the image, you know? At least he thinks so." Dottie looks around for something to use as an ashtray but doesn't find anything, so she flicks her ashes into her opposite palm. "No big deal. I was tired of that scene, anyway. So I started the dogsitting service."

"What happened to it?"

"The business didn't take off."

"It's only been two weeks."

"My landlord wasn't too keen on all the animals in my apartment, and I couldn't pay my bills. So I thought, what the hell? Maybe I'll move home for a while. Aunt Maeve's not getting any younger. I should be closer to her."

"I thought you wanted to act? Or be a dancer or a singer?" Anything that might eventually lead to a role on television or in the movies. Her dream. Just like our mother. "Those kind of jobs are few and far between around here."

A smoke plume rises into the darkness from Dottie's upraised hand. "That's on the back burner for a while. There aren't many of those kind of jobs *anywhere* for middle-aged pregnant women."

For a second, only her expression startles me, not her statement. She looks as if she's bracing for a blow. Then the word *pregnant* sinks in and, suddenly, the crickets are chirping too loud and my heart beats too fast. "You're pregnant?"

"Five and a half months." She leans back in her chair so that I can see her middle across the table. With one hand, she pulls the peasant blouse tight across her stomach. The pooch is small, but it's there. A baby, not the midlife weight I'd thought she'd gained.

Even in the darkness, I catch a glimpse of anxiety

in her eyes. "You're not very big." My focus shifts to the cigarette she holds.

Catching my gaze, Dottie leans down and crushes it out on the patio floor.

"Who's the father?"

"It doesn't matter. He's out of the picture."

I stare up at a sliver of moon. It isn't fair. Why did she come here? To rub in that she's accomplished the one thing I can't? That she's getting what I deserve and she doesn't? I'm sure Aunt Maeve told her about my fertility issues. One thing is certain: she has a lot of nerve. Just as she always did. How am I supposed to feel?

"Why didn't Aunt Maeve tell me?" I ask.

"She didn't know. I didn't tell *her* until I decided to come home last week. We both agreed that I'd be the one to tell you." She takes a sip of tea, sets down the glass and looks me straight in the eye. "I can't keep it."

"What?"

"The kid." She shrugs. "I can't keep it. I have to work all the time just to feed myself. Besides, I don't know anything about taking care of a baby."

After what we went through as children—our mother running off in the middle of the night, our father dumping us with Aunt Maeve—how can she give up her own child and seem so unaffected? So callous?

"I was thinking I'd place it for adoption after it's born," she continues. "But when I told Aunt Maeve, she said you were having trouble getting pregnant, so I thought you might want it."

"You want to *give* me your baby?" A tremor runs through my voice. "Just like that?"

"Why not? I can help you and you can help me. Everyone wins. Simple as that."

My mind races as I push away from the table. Stepping into the yard, my back to Dottie, I close my eyes and take deep breaths. Nothing has changed. She wants me to save her again, as I have since we were little girls. Accept the responsibility for her mistake. Let her off the hook.

After a couple of minutes, Dottie says, "So how about it?"

I don't turn around. "I'm going to have my own baby."

"At your age, don't you think—"

"What I *think* is none of your business."

Her chair legs scrape the concrete. "Well, okay then. Nice seeing you. Maybe we'll run into each other again in another couple of decades."

"Wait!" I swing around. "Have you had anything to eat?"

"I stopped for some chili fries and a Coke a couple of hours ago." Her mouth pulls into a sneer. "What? Don't tell me you're worried about me."

"It's your baby I'm worried about. Somebody should be. There's not a lot of nutrition in chili fries."

Dottie settles a hand across her stomach and lifts her chin. "We're doing okay. Don't lose any sleep over us." She grabs her purse and starts for the door.

"Where are you staying tonight?"

"Aunt Maeve's, I guess."

"You shouldn't drive to Coopersville so late. It's an hour away. You've been on the road for two days. You must be tired."

"Maybe I'll get a room. I'm not *that* broke."

In the time it takes to draw a deep breath, I make a decision. "You can stay here."

She looks at me over her shoulder and says with sarcasm, "I wouldn't want to put you out."

"You won't. I want you to stay. Please."

"Why?"

"For the baby's sake. You'll be more comfortable here than in a motel."

She watches me a minute then says, "Okay. I'll stay. But I'll be out of here first thing in the morning."

CHAPTER 3

At 3:00 a.m. I'm still awake, kicking covers, punching pillows and thinking. About Stan, who hasn't come home. About Dottie, who sleeps in the guest room down the hallway. About her baby and the offer she made.

My sister wants to give me an incredible gift, and my heart goes out to her unborn baby. I already feel a connection to it. Maybe because my mother also left me. But am I the best person to raise my sister's child? I'll always worry that Dottie will show up some day and tell me she's had a change of heart. And even if she didn't, would she expect to be a regular part of our lives? Play the role of the aunt instead of the mother? Could I deal with that?

If Dottie can't provide stability, then adoption is the right choice. I should admire her for recognizing her shortcomings and for not subjecting her child to them. But what I can't understand is her apparent indifference over the life she carries inside of her. She acts as if the baby is a wart she needs to cut off her foot and forget about so she can walk back to her old life with ease.

Dottie is built like our mother. They share the same eyes and mouth, the same complexion. The same dreams. Tonight she confirmed what I guessed all along: their similarities extend even further.

Switching on the lamp, I climb out of bed and head for my dresser to reexamine my other dilemma. The evidence of Stan's betrayal. Maybe finding the bra was a nightmare, an incident I only imagined. That's a ridiculous hope, I know. Still, I pretend there's a chance that the lacy black bra won't be in my lingerie drawer, lying next to one of my conservative, white 34 Bs. Two mountains and a couple of molehills, side by side, reminding me that, once again, I don't measure up.

As I close the drawer, the bedroom door opens and Stan walks in. He pauses when he sees me. "I hope you weren't waiting up."

"I just couldn't sleep."

Tears sting the backs of my eyes as Stan follows me into the bathroom. I know I should confront him about the bra. But I don't have the strength for another emotional scene right now.

We're both quiet as Stan undresses, and I search

the medicine cabinet for aspirin. I find a bottle, wash two tablets down with a glass of water. One question explodes again and again like fireworks in my mind: was he working tonight, or was he with *her*? More than anything, I want to block the images of them together from my thoughts. But it's impossible.

Returning to bed, I turn my back to Stan's side. Seconds later, the mattress shifts as he climbs in next to me. I switch off the lamp, and it occurs to me that, for the past five years, I've been sleeping with a stranger, a man I only thought I knew. Unspoken hurts wedge between us, poking and prodding me, pushing me further and further away from him.

"Dinah?" Stan says when the silence becomes unbearable.

"What?" I say quietly.

"I'm sorry I ruined your birthday."

He doesn't know the half of it. "There'll be other birthdays."

Another long silence, then, "Why do we have a strange dog in our backyard?"

"Oh. That's Hoot Junior."

"Hoot who?"

"My sister's dog. She's here."

"Your sister, Dottie?"

"As far as I know, she's the only sister I have." My

sarcasm slices the air like a knife, reminding me of how Dottie sounds when she's ticked off. I'm ashamed that I'm using anger as a weapon rather than telling Stan what I know, but I can't bring myself to talk to him.

"What's she doing here after—how long did you tell me it's been?"

"Seventeen years."

"And she just showed up? Why?"

"To offer me her baby. She's a little over five months pregnant. If I don't take it, she's giving it up for adoption."

Stan shifts. "You're kidding."

"No."

I swear I hear his mind cranking, processing the information. "Be careful," he finally says. "Don't you think that's fishy? We've been trying to have a baby, then she shows up out of the blue, pregnant, and offers you her kid? What does she want in return? From everything you've told me about her, I wouldn't trust her for a second."

Beneath the covers, I ball my hands into fists and dig my fingernails into my palms. "Don't worry, Stan. I don't trust *anyone* anymore."

Five seconds tick by…ten. Pressure builds in my chest.

"What's wrong?" Stan asks.

"I think I'm getting a migraine," I answer, yearning to turn back the clock, to erase this day and the knowledge it brought me. Wishing he could give me back the one thing that once felt right in my life. My partner. The security of his presence beside me.

His fingers brush the side of my face, hook my hair behind my ear. "I could rub your head for you."

Why does he have to be so nice to me? So tender? I want to hate him right now. To despise the sound of his voice, his scent. Instead those things only make me ache. "I'll be fine."

"You're still mad at me."

"You could say that."

"I've been thinking all night about…" He clears his throat. "We need to talk over some things."

"Not now, Stan. It's been a long day. I just want some sleep. And if our *talk* ended up anything like the one we had earlier, I'm afraid we'd wake up Dottie."

"I'm surprised you let her stay here. I know there's no love lost between the two of you."

I roll onto my back, stare through the darkness toward the ceiling. "She's my sister." Maybe he can't understand the tie that links us, despite our differences. He has no siblings, no living family other than a cousin up north somewhere. Lawrence something-

or-other who left town after they graduated high school, and then dropped off the radar.

"What's your sister like now?" Stan asks.

Dottie's image flashes through my mind, the way she looked today when I first opened the door. The anxiety in her eyes, the relief that followed. I remember our hug and the surprising comfort of having her to lean on.

Another memory from long ago surfaces....

Cooperstown. My first time to meet Aunt Maeve. Daddy's pale face as he climbed into his car. The sound of his voice saying, "I'll be back quick as a whistle, girls. I promise." Dottie and I standing out front of the trailer, watching him drive away, our hands tightly clasped, her tiny fingertips pressing into my palm.

No love lost? I'm not so sure about that. We did love each other. And lost that love somewhere on the path to adulthood. Or maybe it just became so frayed we hid it away, hesitant to examine it for fear it could never be restored.

"You'll see for yourself in the morning what she's like," I tell Stan.

Closing my eyes, I hope for a long night.

Dottie, Stan and I sit at the table eating breakfast. The two of them dance around each another like boxers while I pick at the scrambled eggs Dottie had already made by the time I woke up.

I watch my husband and my sister from beneath lowered lashes. The classified section of the morning newspaper is spread open on the table off to one side of Dottie and, while she eats and talks, she scans the ads.

Stan lifts his steaming coffee mug, his gaze trained on Dottie's face. "So you're looking for work?"

"Yeah." She breaks a strip of bacon in half and tells him about losing her job.

"What other kind of experience do you have?"

The corner of her mouth curls slowly up as she raises her gaze from the newspaper to look at him. When she mimics his narrow-eyed stare, I know she detects the suspicion in his voice. "That depends on what you mean by *experience*."

Stan doesn't flinch. He holds his own in the stare-down, his eyes crinkling at the corners, his mouth quirking slightly on one side. His cop smile. It screams, *I know your game.* "Let's start with work," he says to her.

"Well…" She nibbles the bacon. "Let's see. After I left home and moved to Hollywood I got a job delivering singing telegrams but that didn't pay the bills, so I had a second job as a tap-dancing waitress for a while. In my off hours I auditioned for soaps and com-

mercials. I got a couple of small parts." She slides me
a defensive look, as if daring me to dispute that statement.

According to Aunt Maeve, she was offered *one* part
that never materialized. Still, like the Energizer
Bunny, Dottie kept auditioning, kept going and going
and going in the same old direction toward nowhere.

"Then, when I lived in New York City, I took tickets
at a comedy club, and, oh!" She laughs. "Once I landed
a job as a morgue makeup artist. Everything Aunt
Maeve taught me came in handy on that one. Then in
Vegas? I was a car show hostess once. But before my job
at the casino, I was a live statue at Caesars."

Stan looks as skeptical as I am about all her
oddball jobs. I wonder how much of what she's telling
us is true and how much is fabrication, her limited
acting skills at play.

"I saw a television program about that," Stan says.
"How did you manage to stay still for so long?"

"It wasn't easy. That's why I got fired, as a matter of
fact. One day, I had an itch on my butt that just
wouldn't quit. I knew if I moved I was done for so I
asked the next person who walked by if he'd scratch it."

I butter my toast and wait for the punch line. Dottie
always liked to try to shock people if she thought they
disapproved of her. I have a feeling that hasn't changed.

"Turns out the guy was a Canadian hockey player in town for a tournament," she continues. "Let me tell you, he was more than happy to oblige. What neither of us knew was that my boss, who also happened to be my boyfriend at the time, was across the way watching. So that was that. No more job and no more boyfriend."

Stan's cheek twitches. "That's too bad."

Dottie shrugs. "It worked out fine. I got free tickets to his hockey games and a few more itches scratched, if you know what I mean." Her smile is suggestive. "Which brings us to my *other* kind of experience."

Ignoring her last statement, Stan asks bluntly, "Is the hockey player your baby's father?"

"Are you kidding? I never saw the guy again."

She doesn't seem fazed by that fact, which doesn't surprise me. Hockey players are young and, according to Aunt Maeve, Dottie only falls for older men. Maybe she wants a stand-in for the real daddy who walked out on us. Whatever the case, the hockey player was a fling, a diversion, something to take her mind off the one who got away.

Right now, I wish I could dismiss Stan from my thoughts, from my life, so easily.

"Now the hockey team *owner*...he's another story. He still sends me roses every week." Dottie frowns.

"I'll have to give him my change of address when I get settled. I do love roses."

Stan taps the end of his fork against the table. "You ever been married?"

She makes a scoffing sound. "As far as I'm concerned marriage isn't all it's cracked up to be."

"Why's that?"

"Hasn't Dinah told you how our mama and daddy fought like Tyson and Holyfield before they split?"

Stan sends me an uneasy glance. He knows I hate talking about my parents.

"It's not only them, though," Dottie says. "All the married couples I know are so bored and stale they're growing mold." She cuts her gaze in my direction. "I get so many propositions from guys wearing wedding bands, I can't keep count. Thanks, but no thanks. You can keep your marriage vows."

I'm conflicted by Dottie's turn in the conversation. Uncomfortable, but thankful, too, that she has the guts to try and make Stan squirm. It's good to have someone in my corner, even if that someone is her.

But her inciting comment doesn't seem to affect Stan. He doesn't react, at all. Not a flinch, not a blush, not a blink of the eye.

Why can't I bring myself to ask him if he's having an affair? His reaction, his *answer*, couldn't possibly be any worse than all this self-torture, the imagined scenarios in my head, the questions. Does he find me lacking as a wife? Is he bored with me? Is the other woman smarter than I am? Prettier? Sexier?

I think of last night, before our argument started. He wanted me. He liked the way I looked. But maybe it's all a game to him. An ego stroke. Maybe he derives some perverse sense of power out of juggling two women and getting away with it. At least he *thinks* he's getting away with it.

But none of that sounds like the Stan I know and love. The Stan I *believed* him to be.

He drains the remainder of his coffee then uses a napkin to wipe his mouth. "So where you planning on staying, Dottie? With Maeve in Coopersville?"

She shrugs. "I don't know. Probably. Until the baby's born, anyway."

"Then why are you looking for work here?"

"Aunt Maeve's already told me nobody's hiring in Coopersville. I'll just have to stay with her and make the drive back and forth each day. Or each night, I guess, if I'm waiting tables."

I push back my chair. "Stan, could I talk to you a minute alone before you leave for work?"

"Okay." He stands.

"Y'all don't have to leave the room," Dottie says.

"I could use a smoke. I'll go out to the patio and make sure the dogs have water."

She walks to the counter for her purse, wearing only the long T-shirt she slept in. The slight protrusion of her stomach is more evident this morning than when she wore the blousy peasant top.

Once she's outside, I face Stan. He looks tired. Even so, he's as handsome as ever. Which is my curse, I suppose. Being married to a man who turns women's heads. "I want to ask Dottie to move in with us."

"That's exactly what she's been trying to make happen, can't you see that? She's playing on your sympathy with all that talk of having to make the drive back and forth from Coopersville."

"So? What if she is?"

"She's using you again, like she did when you two were kids. I don't like it. I can see the handwriting on the wall. She moves in, never gets a job and has you waiting on her hand and foot until the baby's born. Or maybe longer. And living free, to boot."

"I've decided to take her up on her offer."

"You mean, adopt her baby?"

"I thought about it all night. It's what I want."

He scrubs a hand across his face, glances away then back to me. "Do you really think it's a good idea to take on your sister's child to raise?"

"Is the ideal situation for having a baby ever going to present itself, Stan? You already told me you're staying in your dangerous job with your crazy hours." *And you're having an affair.* "You're getting everything you want. What about me?"

"We take her baby, we're tied to her for life."

Frustrated, I ask, "Are we even going in the same direction anymore?"

He sighs noisily. "Is this going to be a repeat of yesterday's fight?"

"Tell me one thing, Stan. The other night? When I came up behind you at the computer? You practically jumped out of your skin and almost knocked the monitor over trying to shut it off. Remember?" When he doesn't respond, I continue, "Was that really a case-related e-mail message you were reading, or was it personal?"

His eyes narrow. "I'm not going to waste any more breath on this. You haven't listened to a word I said." Grabbing his jacket from the back of the chair, he says, "I'm going to the station."

I wait until I hear his truck start in the garage, until my breathing steadies, then join Dottie outside. The morning sun warms my skin. A calm breeze blows, but it doesn't soothe me.

Dottie holds the water hose in one hand and a

burning cigarette in the other. Water rushes from the hose into Saxon's bowl, and the two dogs lap it up as it overflows. "Where's Stanny?"

"He left for work."

"Are you sure about that?"

Ignoring her, I walk over and turn off the faucet.

"Cops," Dottie huffs. "Your husband's a regular Barney Fife." She drops the hose and takes a drag off the cigarette. "He was getting off on grilling me, did you notice? I bet you ten bucks he had a hard-on."

Refusing to acknowledge her crude comment, I pick up the hose and wind it around the holder.

"Did you ask him about the bra?"

"That's none of your business."

"Well, I guess that answers my question." She walks to the patio table, sits in a chair, crosses one leg over the other and picks dead grass from the sole of her foot. "Do you love him?"

"That's none of your business, either." Finishing with the hose, I scratch Saxon's head.

"I think you do love the asshole."

I look across at her. "Okay, so I do. What about it?"

She blows out a long stream of smoke, her eyes narrowed. "Are you going to let some double-D slut steal your man?"

My lower lip quivers. I glance toward the fence to

avoid her gaze. "I don't know what I'm going to do, yet, Dottie. But it's not your concern. In case you haven't noticed, you have plenty of your own problems to worry about at the moment."

"Right." She stands up. "Like getting the hell out of here. I get the message."

"That's not what I meant. I don't want you to leave."

"Why?"

"I thought it over last night, and I decided you're right. We can help each other."

Her eyes widen slightly. She sits again. "What are you saying?"

"If you're sure it's what you want, I'd like to raise your baby. But it has to be legal. I'd want us both to see an attorney and have adoption papers drawn up."

"Okay." Turning her head, she takes another drag.

"And, if we're going to do this, I have a few more stipulations."

"Such as?"

I go to her, snatch the cigarette from between her fingers, drop it to the patio floor and smash it with the toe of my house shoe. "No more smoking. And I want you to live here until after the baby is born and you're back on your feet."

"Why? So you can keep an eye on me?"

"Exactly. I'm going to make sure you eat right. No

JENNIFER ARCHER   63

more chili fries. And you'll get plenty of sleep and rest. I'd rather you didn't work."

"So how am I supposed to pay you back for my room and board?"

"You're *giving* me your *child*." Doesn't she realize the enormity of that?

For at least a full minute, she's quiet, studying me. Finally, she nods toward the house. "He's okay with this?"

"He'll come around. And if he doesn't…it's not up to him, anyway. Going into this, you should be aware you're not delivering your baby into the most stable of marriages."

She considers what I've said then sighs. "Your asshole cop husband is gonna be a real joy to live with."

"You think *you're* a joy to live with?"

She tilts her head, smiles a little. "I do my best."

"While you're at it, quit calling him an asshole, would you?"

"I guess macho jerk isn't an option, either, huh?"

I cross my arms and glare.

A slow grin spreads across her face. "I can help you catch Barney in the act. I worked for a P.I. for a couple of years when I lived in New York. I forgot to tell Stanny about that. Besides, if anyone has experience with cheating men, it's me. Of course, *I'm* usually the other woman they're cheatin' with." When I narrow my eyes, she says, "Uh-oh. I shouldn't have said that. I guess it wasn't funny."

"Good guess."

"I'm not proud of some of the things I've done, Dinah. I won't lie about that. But *I* never claimed to be a saint."

I'm more than a little surprised by her admission. I would bet she doesn't give a damn about all the past mistakes she's made or who she hurt making them.

"Not that you ever were, either," she adds. "A saint, that is. Even though you seemed to *think* you had a halo." When I don't respond, Dottie tilts her head back to look me in the eye. "After you get over the shock of finding that bra, you're gonna shove it down his throat, right?"

I know I should. If my life were perfect, a fairy tale or one of the old black-and-white movies my mother used to love, I would be the strong confident heroine. I would march right up to Stan with the big black bra and ask, "Hey, what's this?" Then everything would work out fine. But even though I've left Coopersville behind, the pain of my childhood, the shame I used to feel, it turns out my life is as perfectly imperfect as it ever was.

CHAPTER 4

Dottie

Hey, Peep. Mission accomplished; I thought you'd want to know.

Dinah will be a good mother. She's everything I'm not.

I guess you're curious about her. Let's see… what can I tell you? Well, sometimes you'd think she has a corncob up her butt, but I have a feeling she's more easygoing when I'm not around. And she can be a little holier-than-thou. Okay, a *lot* holier-than-thou. At least with me. But since she's going to be your mom, I should probably focus on the positives.

Hmm. Positives. Surely there's something…

The truth is, she took care of me when we were girls. That never really sank in until I found out I was going to have a kid, and I started thinking about being a kid myself. As far back as I could remember, Dinah was there. Fixing my meals, making sure I took a bath and that I got to school on time, getting me out of trouble whenever I got into it—which was a lot. Sometimes she even covered for me or took the blame to save my butt, though it grated on her and she always yelled at me afterward.

Aunt Maeve was good to us but, like me and your grandma, she wasn't mother material. At least not the perfect kind you see in old TV shows like June on *Leave It to Beaver* or what's-her-name on *The Brady Bunch*. If me or Dinah needed her, she'd be there for us. Otherwise, she pretty much left us to fend for ourselves. Aunt Maeve had a business to tend to.

No question about it, Dinah got the responsible gene in the family, which is a good trait for a mother to have, I guess. Even if it does sometimes make her come off like a Sunday school teacher at a beer bust. But she'll love you. More than anything. She'll do everything to give you a nice life.

Speaking of nice, you should see your new neighborhood. Dinah would've had fancier if she'd married the lawyer. But don't get me wrong, this place is no dump. The streets are lined with little prim boxes, all in a row. Kids skateboard on the sidewalks and shoot baskets in the driveways. The air smells like barbecue. I'm surprised there's not a flag flying in every yard; it's that kind of place. Great for you to grow up in, but I wouldn't be able to breathe here after more than a couple of months. I'm allergic to potluck block parties, church socials and good-old-fashioned family values.

Right now I'm trying to catch a nap in Dinah's guest room since she got it in her head I should rest twice a day—late morning and late afternoon. This is my room until you're born. After that I guess it'll be *your* room. You'll like it, Peep. It has a big window overlooking the backyard, pale-yellow walls and cream-colored carpet so thick it squishes between my toes.

If I were fixing it up for you, I'd add a wallpaper border. Maybe sailboats if you're a boy and rainbows if you're a girl. And I'd put your crib—

Well, that's Dinah's problem, not mine. I don't get into cutsie, anyway.

The only drawback to this setup I can see is Mr. Look-At-Me-I'm-A-Tough-Detective. I'm hoping there's something worthwhile buried underneath his macho bullshit. I'm also hoping somebody stuffed that bra in his pocket as a joke, for Dinah's sake.

And yours.

CHAPTER 5

Dinah

Yesterday I helped Dottie move a few things from her U-Haul to the guest room. Then I called a storage facility and rented a small space for her washer, dryer and furniture.

Today, I work on my magazine article until eleven, then sit back and stare at the screen, unable to concentrate. When a knock sounds, I glance over my shoulder.

Dottie stands in the doorway, watching me.

I swivel around to face her. "Come in. I could use a break."

She sinks into the chair across from my desk, looking bored and as wrung out as a string mop. She doesn't wear the false eyelashes today. Mascara smudges the space beneath her left eye. "I walked the dogs. I watched two morning talk shows. I even tried to take a nap to make you happy, but I'm not sleepy. I'm going stir-crazy."

"It's only your second day here. Give it some time.

We'll figure out something to keep you busy. Something nonstressful."

"Like what? Your neighbor's Tupperware party? I saw the invitation." Her lip curls. "Sitting around burping the air out of plastic bowls sounds like a wild time to me. I can hardly wait."

"We could rent some old movies. You still like them, don't you?"

"Yeah, but not twenty-four hours a day."

She lays a hand across her stomach, and I notice a sheen of perspiration on her face. "Are you feeling okay?"

"Other than the fact that I'm melting?"

"It's probably hormonal. The house feels cool enough to me. When was the last time you saw a doctor?"

"More than a month ago. I missed my last appointment. My boss wouldn't let me off."

"I'll call my gynecologist and get you in. She delivers babies. I think you'll like her." I look at Dottie's stomach and mine flutters with a combination of nervousness and excitement. A hint of jealousy, too. "Have you had a sonogram?"

"Yeah. Just to make sure the baby was okay. You know, because of my age."

"Did they say what the sex is?"

"It was too soon to tell. I didn't want to know, anyway."

Do I only imagine a hint of sadness in her eyes? Maybe she's afraid knowing the baby's sex will make it more difficult for her to let go. But that can't be; everything she's said, every action she's taking, confirms that she feels no bond with her child.

"If you want to know, that's fine," she says. "I'll leave it up to you. It doesn't make me any difference."

"I'll think about it."

"Sure. Whatever you want." She looks past me to the computer screen and scoots to the edge of her chair. "So what's the plan?"

"The plan?"

"For uncovering the identity of Stan's harlot."

My stomach flip-flops. "I don't have a plan. I'm not sure I want to know."

Dottie lifts a brow. "So you're gonna let him screw around with her then come home and pretend he's had a rough day?"

"I guess I'd like a little more ammunition before I start accusing him." Or maybe I'd rather pretend I never found that bra so I won't have to deal with it. I want to believe there's an innocent explanation. I'm afraid of the truth, afraid hearing it will mark the beginning of the end of our marriage.

Dottie leans forward, and I can tell by the sneaky look in her eyes that I should run now before she coerces me into something I'll regret. "Let's tap into his e-mail."

Every cell in my body rebels at the idea. "I couldn't do anything like that. It seems so...I don't know... sleazy and wrong."

"And screwing around isn't?" She tilts her head, squints at me. "You want answers, or not?"

"Yes, but—" Pushing aside my ethics and anxiety, I swallow and nod once. "Okay. But how? I'm not a hacker."

"What mail server does he use?"

"I'm not sure. Yahoo!, I think."

She smiles. "Good. That means all we need is his user name and password, and we can check his mail from any computer."

"I know his user name. I've seen him type it in. It's Hager plus our zip code." Feeling queasy, I recite the numerals.

Standing, Dottie lifts her chair.

"Put that down! I'll move it."

"I'm not sick, I'm knocked up." She carries the chair around the desk and sets it down beside mine so that we can both see the computer screen. "What about his password?"

"I don't know. When he types that in, it isn't visible." I face the monitor, place my fingers on the keyboard, my palms sweating as I tap the keys. Seconds later, the Yahoo! sign-in page comes up. I start to type Stan's user name into the appropriate box, then pause and glance over my shoulder, terrified I'll find him beneath the doorway watching me, though he's never home this time of day. Of course, he isn't there, so I turn back to the screen, my hand shaking as I hit the tab key. The cursor moves to the password box and blinks at me. "Now what?"

"We only get three tries, I think, and then they lock you out, so let's start with the obvious. What's his mother's maiden name?"

"Pinkersly." I type the name in. Nothing.

"Hmm. Try your name." Before I can, she catches my wrist and smirks. "On second thought, he'd probably be more likely to choose supercop or *Dirty Harry* or something like that."

"Funny, Dottie." I type in the month, day and year of his birthday, instead.

When that doesn't work, Dottie leans back in her chair, puffs out her cheeks then says, "What's his favorite movie?"

"I don't have a clue."

"His favorite color?"

"As far as I know, he doesn't have one." I sigh.

"This is hopeless. And it's *wrong*." She frowns at me and opens her mouth to speak, but before she utters a word, I say, "I know, I know. So is an affair."

"You've gotta drop the Pollyanna bit. This is war. Try your dog's name."

I type in "Saxon." Voilá. "Oh my gosh!"

Dottie's smile is smug.

Crossing my arms, I give her a look, half scowl, half grin. "You should consider computer hacking as another job option."

Her brow wrinkles, as if she's considering it.

"I hope you know I'm kidding."

We both return our focus to the screen and the list of messages that fill Stan's in-box. One subject header stands out to me. It reads lunch on Wednesday the 7th, and the sender's name is Lou Lou. The message was sent yesterday. I point at it. "Look at this."

Dottie tucks a limp lock of hair behind her ear. "The lunch date's today. Let's see what it says."

I position the arrow over the message, hold my breath and click, then read silently.

Hi there Stan,
Are we still having lunch tomorrow? If so, how about Zen at noon? I'll dress up for you. Once you see me out in public you'll realize how easy this can

be and maybe you'll feel more comfortable. I'll even wear my new pink shoes. You're going to love them.

See you soon,

Lou Lou

"Bingo," Dottie murmurs.

I squeeze the mouse so tight I'm surprised it doesn't squeal. "She'll dress up for him. *She'll dress up for him.*" Banging my fist on the desktop, I say, "I hate this woman. I hate her. *Lou Lou.* What kind of name is that? A stripper's name, that's what kind. She's probably an exotic dancer. Oh my God! *Oh my God!* He could get a disease. *I* could get a disease."

Dottie surprises me by wrapping an arm around my shoulder. "I'm thinking they haven't been at this long since they've never gone out in public together. That's good. It means we have a chance of putting a stop to things before they get more serious."

"And before someone I know sees him and I'm completely humiliated."

"That's what's eatin' you?" Lowering her arm, she huffs and says, "You haven't changed. Always worrying about what people think."

I don't waste time defending myself. Knowing Dottie, it would only spiral into an argument.

"The message isn't very sexy," she says. "They must be having the most boring affair in the history of adultery."

"Stan wouldn't be drawn to a hopeless romantic," I mutter. What I don't say, is that he's also not boring. We may have problems, but boredom's not one of them. Especially in bed. The woman may not be getting hearts and flowers, but if she's sleeping with my husband, she's getting something better. Something that only *I* should be getting. And that makes me want to put my fist through the monitor and snatch Lou Lou out of Stan's in-box. Out of his life.

Settling one forearm across her middle, Dottie props her opposite elbow on it and rests her chin in her hand. She stares at the screen. "What kind of woman do you picture when you read that?"

Uncertain where she's going with the question, I reread the e-mail then say, "A big-busted, bald-headed woman?"

She scowls. "*Bald*-headed?"

"After I tear all her hair out."

Her mouth curves up at one corner. "Good. It's about time you got good and pissed off."

"So, why did you ask me that?"

Dottie frowns. "I'm not sure. Check out his Sent

file. If he saves the e-mails he sends out, we might find his message back to her."

The message is there, as Dottie suspected. The date indicates that he e-mailed her last night. "That's strange. I figured they were together then." I click on the message, lean forward to read it.

Hey,
I'll meet you for lunch, but Zen is too crowded, especially at noon. I might see somebody I know. There's a Chinese place off the Boulevard called Wong's. Let's make it one o'clock.
See you then,
Stan

While I fume, Dottie glances at her watch. "It's almost one o'clock now. You hungry?"

"Yes, but we can't eat at Wong's. I'm not ready for a confrontation, especially with *her.*"

"I didn't mean we'd eat there. We can drive-through somewhere on the way, grab a burger and eat in the car."

"On the way *where?*"

"To Wong's." Dottie sounds exasperated that I'm slow to catch on to this investigating business. "We'll park somewhere close by and watch the door." When I hesitate, she says, "Don't you want to at least get a glimpse of her?"

Maybe I should give him the benefit of the doubt. Wait a few days and then recheck his messages before jumping to conclusions. Or maybe I should just confess to him that I read the e-mails and give him a chance to explain. But I have a feeling the first option would only postpone the inevitable, while the second would only gain me more excuses and evasiveness from Stan.

Again, I read the message he wrote to Lou Lou. With each word, my anger intensifies. I refuse to make light of the evidence that's right in front of my face. I won't be a wimp, sit back and hope everything will work out. One way or another, I'm going to find out what Stan's doing behind my back. And with whom.

I log off the computer, push back my chair. "Come on."

Dottie moves fast for a pregnant woman. She's out of her chair in an instant. "Let's go see what's attached to those double D's."

Thirty minutes later, I park my blue Honda Accord in a used car dealership lot at the opposite corner from Wong's. We have a clear view of the café door and parking lot. Stan's black truck sits there, alongside a white Audi. There is a silver minivan, too, a red motorcycle and a powder-blue LTD.

Outside, it's cloudy and muggy. I leave the car running for the air-conditioning and settle in to wait. In silence, Dottie and I eat, both staring at the café entrance. Every few seconds she grumbles under her breath. At the fast-food place we stopped at on the way, I insisted we order grilled chicken salads instead of hamburgers, bottled water rather than soft drinks, and no fries. She wasn't thrilled.

After about five minutes, a tap sounds on my window. I jump, dropping my plastic fork and the binoculars. Dottie gasps and snaps the camera. A car salesman whose name tag reads Wayne peers in at us. I roll the window down and the scent of rain drifts in.

"You ladies need some help?"

"Oh, um…" I smile at him. "Not really. Do you mind if we sit here a while? We won't bother anything."

He scratches his head. "I'm not sure the boss would go for that."

Dottie leans across the seat and looks out at him, offering a direct view of her cleavage. "Hi, there." She gives him the same flirty smile she used on the football jocks back in high school. "You don't mind if I call you Wayne, do you?"

"No, ma'am." He stands a little straighter and adjusts his tie.

"I'd like to meet your boss," she says. "Would you introduce me?"

"Is there a problem?"

"Oh, no." She laughs. "No problem at all. We don't want to cause you any trouble."

He thinks things over, then shrugs. "Come on. I'll take you to him."

Dottie sets her salad on the dash and climbs from the car. As they walk away, I hear her talking in a sugary voice. Wayne chuckles, and she laughs, too.

I roll up my window, refocus the binoculars on Wong's front door, and continue to eat from the disposable container in my lap. An elderly couple walk out and drive away in the LTD. The sky begins to spit rain on my windshield.

Soon, Dottie returns. "We can stay here as long as we like," she says, closing her door.

Without lowering the binoculars, I ask, "What did you say to him?"

"I said—"

"There's Stan!" He steps out the front door of Wong's, tips his head back to look at the sky, then turns back to the doorway and speaks to someone inside the café.

"Does this camera have a zoom lens?" Dottie whispers.

"Push the tab to the right of the button," I whisper back.

A tall woman steps through the café doorway and joins Stan. I hope my binoculars are faulty because, from what I can see, she is drop-dead gorgeous despite her size. Not that she's fat; she isn't. She's the Amazon I imagined. My worst nightmare come true. Her long, pale blond hair is sleek and straight, pulled back into a smooth ponytail, revealing a striking face with prominent cheekbones. She wears a flared brown skirt, a silky pink blouse, matching pink pointy-toed shoes. Her legs are as long as the string of curse words I'd like to shout.

Dottie whistles quietly. "She makes two of you."

"Two improved versions, maybe." I lower my plastic fork to the container as the salad dressing I've consumed sours in my stomach. "I was hoping the rest of her would match the circumference of her chest. She's beautiful."

"She's okay if you like the cool Swedish type."

I slump back against the seat, feeling as plain and exciting as a brown paper bag. "Somehow, the name Lou Lou painted a different picture in my mind."

"Look at it this way." Dottie lowers the camera to glance at me. "If she looked like a bulldog it would be a slap in the face."

"It would?"

"Yeah. Why would Stanny want someone like that when he could have you?"

"That really cheers me up, Dottie. Since she *doesn't* look like a bulldog, now the question is why would Stan want someone like *me* when he can have *her?*"

Dottie lifts the camera again and aims it at Stan and the other woman. "Pink with brown is *so* last year," she whispers, snapping away like the paparazzi. "And that frigid housewife hairstyle went out half a decade ago, at least."

If I weren't overcome with jealousy and rage, I'd be amused by Dottie's attempt to console me.

The woman raises an umbrella. Stan slips sunglasses on and follows her to the sidewalk, out of the way of the door, where they face each other and talk.

Dottie sighs. "It looks like the bra would fit her."

"Why are we whispering? They're half a block away."

Stan starts to turn away from the blonde, but before he does, she moves closer and hugs him.

Their embrace strangles me. Closing my eyes, I say, "Tell me when that—that…home wrecking *witch* takes her hands off my husband."

"I told you he's an ass—" Dottie shrieks as a knock sounds on her side of the car.

I scream, too.

Cursing, she lowers her window.

Wayne stands outside holding two soft drink cans. "Here are those Cokes you asked for." He gives them to Dottie, then puts his hands in his pockets and stares across the way at Wong's. "See anything interesting over there?"

"Oh, you'd be surprised," Dottie says, then thanks him for the drinks and sends him on his way.

I take a can. "I thought we agreed you'd cut down on the junk?"

"You can't expect me to go cold turkey on *every* vice."

"What *did* you say to his boss?" Dottie wiggles her brows and, when she starts to answer, I say, "On second thought, I don't want to know."

Holding the can in one hand, I lift the binoculars with the other. Stan and the woman no longer stand on the sidewalk. His truck pulls out of the parking lot. The motorcycle follows with Lou Lou riding it, a helmet covering her head, her skirt flapping around her knees. The buckles on her pink shoes shine in the sun.

I grab my sunglasses from the overhead compartment, slam them onto my face, and duck down in the seat as they pass by. "*Look* at her."

Coke spews out Dottie's nose. But when she sees my tears aren't from laughter, she sobers and wipes her eyes.

"Is that the kind of woman he wants? Someone more adventurous than me? Is that what she gives him that I don't?"

"Lou Lou is the flavor of the week, Di, that's all. Men like variety. That's what I think, anyway. What do *you* think?"

"I think I want to go hear what Stan has to say about his lunch date."

"You sure you're ready for that?"

"I'm going to have to face him sooner or later."

A horn blares behind us, and we both jump. Coke and salad flies everywhere as we turn to look out the back window. Stan's truck sits behind us.

Dottie winces. "Looks like sooner," she says.

CHAPTER 6

As Stan strides toward the car, I feel like an entire head of lettuce is lodged in my throat.

"You want to tell me what you're doing?" he asks after I roll down my window. He jerks the sunglasses off his face.

I take mine off, too. "Who is she, Stan?"

"Who are you talking about?"

"The woman you had lunch with."

He pales. "So now you're *following* me?"

"You didn't answer my question."

Leaning down, he looks across at Dottie. "Let me guess. This was *her* idea, wasn't it?"

"It doesn't matter whose idea it was."

"I'm not talking about this with an audience."

"Fine." I glance at my sister. "I'll be right back."

Her brows lift. "Take your time." She turns on the radio and cranks up the volume. "Don't Go Breaking My Heart" blares from the speakers.

Brushing salad from my lap with Coke-sticky

fingers, I follow Stan to the back of the car. Rain still sprinkles down from a dreary sky.

Stan squints at me. "What the hell's going on, Dinah?"

"That's what I'd like to know." I cross my arms. "I found the bra, Stan."

"You—" He flinches.

"In your jacket pocket last night after you walked out."

"So not only are you stalking me, you're searching my pockets, too. Is that it?"

"Don't you dare try to turn this around and make me the bad guy. It was hanging out of your pocket. If you wanted to get away with cheating, maybe you should've been more careful to hide the evidence."

Brakes squeal nearby. Neither of us looks over to the road; we keep our gazes on each other as the rain begins to fall harder. "I'm not cheating on you," Stan finally says.

"Do you really expect me to believe that? Why else would you have a bra in your pocket?"

He looks down at the wet pavement, stares in silence at it for so long I start to wonder if he's gone mute.

"Oh, I get it. This is one of those things you can't discuss with your wife, right? You must think I'm a complete idiot. It's a big bra and that was a big woman I just saw you with."

"The bra isn't—" He curses under his breath and blurts a laugh that intensifies my outrage; I can't decide if he's frustrated or amused.

"No wonder you don't want to go into business with Pete anymore. It would limit your coming and going. I'd know right where to find you every day. You wouldn't be able to pretend you're working late on a case when you're really with that...that... blond *biker* bitch in cheap Manolo Blahnik knock-offs."

Stan blinks repeatedly. The ends of his hair are starting to curl from the moisture in the air. I've never seen his face so red. Jamming his hands into his pants' pockets, he opens his mouth then closes it and looks away.

"Aren't you going to defend yourself?"

"Dinah..." His Adam's apple shifts. "I know this looks bad, but you're just going to have to trust me."

"Quit saying that! How *can* I trust you?"

"A better question might be how can you trust *her?*" He nods toward the front of the car where Dottie sits, moving her shoulders and head to the music on the radio. "You haven't seen her in almost twenty years. She treated you like shit, yet you fall in line with her plans when she drops back into your life." He snaps his fingers. "Just like that."

"Dottie's not the issue here. Don't try to change the subject."

"I'm trying to protect you. I ran a rap sheet on her, Dinah. Your sister has so many hot checks on her record she could wallpaper the police station with them. If she got stopped they'd haul her ass into jail so fast she wouldn't know what hit her. I should haul her in myself. You're the only reason I'm not."

Thunder rumbles. "How dare you check out my sister." I glance at the back of Dottie's head, which still bops side-to-side. It doesn't matter that I'm ambivalent in trusting her, Stan has no right to go behind my back to look into her past. Yes, I went behind *his* back and read his e-mail but, because of his lies, I tell myself I'm justified.

"Considering her track record," Stan says, "how do you know she's not dangling this baby in front of you to get something she wants? After she gets it, she could just disappear from your life again and take the baby with her."

When Dottie told me she was pregnant, I thought the same thing. That she was after something. But in less than two days, everything has changed, and I refuse to consider that possibility; I don't want to. I already ache to hold her baby in my arms. My baby. My little boy or girl. "She hasn't asked me for a thing," I say quietly, listening to the music that drifts from Dottie's window, to the patter of raindrops on the pavement.

"She didn't have to. You gave it all to her on a silver platter. Just like she hoped you would. She knows you have a soft heart. And don't you think Maeve told her we've been trying to have a baby and it hasn't happened?"

Aunt Maeve *did* tell her that. Dottie admitted as much. Uncertainty and suspicion creep up on me, but I refuse to let them grab hold. "What would Dottie want from me?"

"A meal ticket until the baby's born. A free place to live. No worries about having to hold down a job. Did you offer to pay her medical bills?" When I avert my gaze, he says, "That's what I thought. You probably plan to buy baby clothes, right? Toys? Plenty of stuff for her to take along when she and her kid disappear."

Silent sobs heave my chest. I hold them back, breathe in, breathe out. Again and again. The scent of diesel fumes in the air sickens me.

Stan's eyes soften. "I'm afraid she'll break your heart again," he says. "Only it'll be worse this time because a child is involved."

"You're the one breaking my heart, Stan. You've

invented this whole scenario about Dottie to try to overshadow your own betrayal."

"I didn't—" His jaw muscle twitches. "I know this looks bad. I know I'm hurting you, and I'm sorry for that. But I can explain everything. The bra... that—" Blushing again, he cuts a glance toward Wong's. "I can explain," he repeats. "I just can't do it now. Give me some time."

He reaches for my arm.

I jerk it back. "I'm not going to wait around for you to make up some excuse. I thought about leaving you the other night, did you know that? You asked me if I was bailing and I almost said yes. I thought maybe we needed some time apart to decide if we want the same things. But I changed my mind because I love you. I want our marriage to work. Then I found that bra, and..." My voice quivers. I turn away, watch the cars pass by on the Boulevard, all the people inside of them oblivious that the world is shattering. "I want our marriage to work," I repeat in a whisper. "We can finally have the family we've always wanted. Don't throw that away." I meet his gaze. "Please tell me what's going on with you. We can talk to a counselor and work through it."

"Why won't you listen to me?" Frustration raises his voice an octave. "We don't *need* to talk to a counselor."

"Then talk to *me*, Stan."

Hesitation flickers across his face, as if he's considering it. But it snuffs out quickly, as if drowned by the rain, his own stubbornness, some insecurity or fear I can't comprehend.

"Maybe you were right the other night," he says. "Maybe we could use some time apart."

The impact of his statement knocks the breath from my lungs.

"Baby or not, I'm afraid I'm never going to be able to give you the kind of life you want. Until I'm too old to do otherwise, I'll work long hours at a dangerous job. That's just how it is. I'd be miserable doing anything else. I should give you some space to think about that, to decide if you can live with it. If you even *want* to."

It seems as if we stand there forever, facing each another, avoiding each other's eyes.

"I'll get my things from the house and stay at Pete's," Stan finally says.

Before I can respond, Wayne ambles over and asks, "Y'all need anything?"

"We're fine," Stan snaps without looking at the man.

Wayne scratches his head and frowns. "Is he bothering you, lady?"

"I *said*, we're *fine*." Stan turns to him briefly and flashes his badge.

"No problem." Wayne straightens, clearing his throat. Then, with a wave to Dottie, he walks away.

"So this is it?" I ask. "We end our marriage in a used car parking lot?"

He scrapes a hand across his hair. "We're not ending our marriage. I told you...we just need some space for a while. I think you were right about that."

"And I told *you*, I changed my mind."

Another long silence. "You want me to call before I come by for my things?"

"I—" My throat tries to close. "It doesn't matter. You don't have to call. Come whenever you want."

With a nod, he returns to his truck and leaves me standing alone.

On the way home, Dottie and I don't talk; I can't bring myself to say anything.

That evening, I feel the mattress shift but don't lift my head from the pillow or open my eyes. Earlier, I let Saxon up on the bed with me. I bury my face in his soft neck and cling to him.

"Hi." Dottie's voice is quiet and hesitant. "If Stan is leaving you because of me or our plans for the baby, I'll go right now."

"No." I release Saxon, open my eyes and look up. "It's not about you. Oh, he tried to turn it into that to cover for himself, but we were in trouble before you got here."

"I'm not up for ending another one of your relationships."

Our gazes lock, and I wonder if she feels the same pang of regret that I do for the years we've missed.

"That was a long time ago," I say. Sitting up, I lean back against the pillows. "I don't see any point in rehashing it. Blaine would've ended the engagement sooner or later, anyway. His parents would have pressured him to. I didn't fit into their circle, and they knew it."

The Medfords didn't have to meet Dottie to guess the truth. Maybe my background was evident in the way I walked or talked, in the sound of my voice, the look in my eye. I used to wonder about all that, worry about it, but I stopped caring a long time ago.

"Besides, he wasn't right for me. Stan's the love of my life." I huff a stale laugh. "Or so I thought. Anyway, you don't have to apologize for breaking up Blaine and me."

There was a time when I blamed her for that…and for more. If I'd married Blaine, I'd probably have a son or a daughter right now. A teenager, most likely. But what stung the most, what still stings, wasn't that her actions ended my relationship with Blaine, but the fact that she wanted to hurt me. After all I'd done for her, she'd thought so little of me. That's what she should apologize for.

Dottie looks at me straight-on. "I wasn't going to apologize."

"Oh." I feel myself blush. *I should've known.* We stare at each other.

"What I did was lousy, but what you did was just as bad."

A rush of air leaves my lungs. This must be "Beat-up Dinah Day." "I'll admit that I was wrong when I didn't tell you and Aunt Maeve about my engagement. And you should've both been there when we announced it."

"You made her feel like trash."

Shame washes over me. "Aunt Maeve said that?"

"She didn't have to. I saw it on her face. If you wanted to snub me, fine. But not her. She didn't deserve it. When we got dumped, she took us in and took care of us."

I bristle. "*I* took care of us."

"You—" She closes her mouth and frowns then reaches across me to ruffle Saxon's fur. "Forget it. You've got enough on your plate."

A part of me wants to continue the conversation,

to get every hurtful thing out in the open on the same day and be done with it. My problems with Stan, my problems with my sister. I remember the last thing she said to me on that night seventeen years ago before we parted ways and went on to lives that didn't include each another.

You stopped being my sister a long time ago.

So much pain in that statement. So much pain in her expression when she spoke it. Pain too deep to have come only from that one incident.

But how could she feel that *I'd* wronged *her*? It wasn't fair. Growing up, I resented her, yes. She demanded too much from me. From the time we came to Aunt Maeve's, even before that. When our mother wouldn't make the effort to do the things Dottie needed her to do.

Over the years, how many homework assignments did I help her complete, did I complete *for* her, when she'd put them off until late the night before they were due? Who took the blame for the pack of cigarettes found in her locker when she was in sixth grade and a third strike would've meant school suspension? Who told Aunt Maeve that fifteen-year-old Dottie was asleep in bed at 11:00 p.m., then drove to Amarillo at three in the morning to pick her up when she called from a party, slobber-slinging drunk?

Who cleaned her up and kept her secret after she had a miscarriage at sixteen?

I *was* there for her. Always. Her sister. More than her sister.

Until that night in Austin.

"You're right," I tell her now. "This isn't the best time to reopen old wounds."

But I do want to open them. Soon. Before Dottie disappears from my life for another seventeen years.

CHAPTER 7

The next day, Dottie drags into my office. Overnight, her stomach seems to have grown from the size of a cantaloupe to a small watermelon. First thing this morning, I called my doctor. The soonest she could get Dottie in was on Monday.

"Let's go to Coopersville," she says in her don't-mess-with-me voice.

"I told you I can't go until tomorrow. I have to finish this article." With a sinking feeling in my stomach, I frown at the blank page on my computer screen.

"Finish it? Have you even started? You're not fooling me. You haven't written a word in the past couple of days."

"I can't focus on it," I admit, sighing. "I can't afford to lose this assignment." Especially if I have to support a baby without Stan's help. In which case, I'll have to freelance during the school year, too. Raising a child on a teacher's salary alone would be challenging, at best.

"What's one more day?" Crossing one leg over the other, Dottie wiggles her toes. Chipped, pale orange polish coats her toenails. "It's so gloomy around here, even Hoot's draggin' his butt around. What we all need is a dose of Aunt Maeve."

I start to say that's the last thing I need then change my mind. Maybe I feel guilty, I don't know. But after our talk last night, I do want to see my aunt. Reaching for the phone, I say, "Okay, I'll go. Let me give her a call."

"Why don't we surprise her?"

I put down the receiver. "I'm a little afraid of what we might interrupt. Apparently, Grady Jarvis has been spending a lot of time at her place. And not to have his tea leaves read, either."

Dottie shrieks. "Not the Grady Jarvis who graduated with you! The football jock?"

"One and the same."

She shrieks again. "That would make him forty years old. Aunt Maeve is sixty. Who told you they were doing the dirty deed?"

"She did. I'm surprised she didn't tell you, too. She can't figure out what all the fuss is with the people in town."

"And doesn't give a rat's ass, I bet."

"Of course not. When did she ever care what anybody thought about her?"

Except for Dottie and me. Aunt Maeve cared what we thought. But I was too insensitive to see that. As a kid, I cringed whenever my friends were around her, whenever they saw where we lived, how she earned our keep.

I roll away from my desk. "We should stop by the bakery and pick up some chocolate éclairs."

Dottie tilts her head and gives me a funny look. "You knew those are her favorites?"

"I lived with her for ten years, didn't I?"

"I didn't think you paid attention." She smiles. "Remember that time she tried to whip some up from scratch? Holy smoke, the woman can't scramble an egg. I don't know how she thought she could make éclairs. The filling was thin as milk."

"I think she's the only one who doesn't know she's a bad cook."

"She's still baking for her customers?"

"All the time. Every Dumpster in Coopersville is probably full of her efforts."

We laugh together over our aunt, and it strikes me that I've found humor in what once embarrassed me. I realize, too, that I can't remember the last time my sister and I had a carefree conversation. Did we ever? If so, it was long ago. Too long. Our ease with one another today feels good. So good I don't want it to end. I don't want to think about unresolved problems. I don't want to waste another minute of time worrying because Stan hasn't called, or spend another second hoping the reason he hasn't come by for his things is because he's changed his mind about leaving. Something tells me I'd only be setting myself up for another letdown.

I turn off the computer. "Aunt Maeve's going to ask me about Stan. I'd rather not talk about what's going on with us. What should I tell her?"

Dottie makes a scoffing sound. "You know her sixth sense about trouble. She'll guess if you're keeping something from her."

She's right. During the first weeks after Dottie's miscarriage when she was sixteen, Aunt Maeve kept asking me what was wrong. I thought Dottie and I were covering well, but Aunt Maeve saw through the facade all the way to my sister's bruised heart. When I wouldn't tell her anything, she finally guessed the truth. And then they cried together. Rocked and cried while I looked on, wounded because I was the one who had been there for Dottie, but we couldn't bring ourselves to hold one another. By that time, our mutual resentment was already too strong.

"Better go ahead and drop the bomb about Stan and be done with it." Suddenly, Dottie sits straighter and flattens a palm against her stomach.

Alarmed, I lean toward her. "Is something wrong?"

"Feel this." She takes my hand, lifts hers and puts mine beneath it. "Wait a minute."

Holding my breath, I stare at our fingers, spread wide across her tight belly.

"Feel it?"

I do. A tiny thump followed by a gentle wavelike movement over her middle from left to right, as if, inside her, the baby slides a fist from one hip bone to the other.

For the first time since I agreed to Dottie's offer, it's real to me. The baby. The fact that I'll soon be a mother. Awe fills my body, as the baby fills hers. Love for the child, gratitude to my sister. A certainty that I'll never be able to repay her for what she's giving me. Does she even realize how much it means?

When I look up, her eyes are closed. "Thank you," I whisper.

Dottie squeezes my hand. She doesn't open her eyes.

Dottie insists we take Hoot and Saxon. They sit in the back of the Accord on top of a beach towel I spread across the seat. Hoot is the impatient juvenile, panting, pacing and pawing at the window. Frustrated whines tremble from his throat. *Are we there yet?*

Saxon, wise and long-suffering, stays on his side

and quietly stares out at the passing scenery, ignoring Hoot's petulance.

Beside me, Dottie fidgets and chatters while I drive the knife-straight highway that slices the flat land between Amarillo and Coopersville into matching left and right pieces. She hasn't made this drive in years, and nothing escapes her notice.

"Isn't that a new barn at the old Ridgeway brothers' farm, or did they just paint the old one?"

She points out an old-fashioned red hay barn across the field alongside us, a fresh, bright speck of color against the sun-blanched grass. "I don't know, I've never noticed." Each time I make this drive alone, I'm focused on getting to Coopersville, not the scenery, eager to do my duty, get it over with and return home.

"I bet the old coots made a killing when the state bought their land to widen the road."

"If so, it wasn't the Ridgeways who got rich. Aunt Maeve said they sold out years ago to some other farmer."

"Who'd they sell to?"

"I can't remember. All I know is the reconstruction took forever."

We drive another mile…two, past cornfields and grazing cattle.

Dottie's face scrunches up as we approach a feed

yard. "Whew! I'd forgotten that smell. Those cows stink worse than Hoot's breath."

"I'm not so sure about that."

Coopersville pops onto the landscape like an afterthought, a project begun in haste then discarded. A scatter of gray buildings on the outskirts of town. A feed store. A farm equipment supplier. A couple of gas stations and an auto body shop.

"It's good to be back," Dottie says, and I take a closer look, trying to see the place as she does, to understand what's good about being here, what might possibly warrant the sentimentality I hear in her voice.

When I reach the flashing yellow light announcing the town's first intersection, I turn left off the highway onto a road that soon becomes Main.

Christmas lights from six months ago still adorn the courthouse's upper perimeter, their twinkle extinguished. The twisted cord sags over some of the windows, making the tired stone building resemble a jilted old woman, all dressed up and still waiting on her date long after the bartender's last call.

At the far edge of town, I swing right into Ponderosa Mobile Home Park. Dirt swirls on the unpaved road as we inch past rusty trailers lined up like shabby, fallen tin soldiers beside stamp-size yards they once guarded.

We stop on the curve of a cul-de-sac in front of a peeling white sign painted in deep purple script that reads:

> MADAME MAEVE'S
> Hair & Wig Styling
> Manicures, Makeup & Tea Leaf Readings
> Drop-ins Welcome

Behind the sign, a double-wide trailer sits askew on a larger lot than those of its neighbors, demanding attention with its dark-purple door and matching shutters; the Queen Bee of the Ponderosa. Silver Lace vine spirals through the chain-link fence, a tangled snake, trapped by its own efforts to wander and climb.

On the porch, Babe, Aunt Maeve's big poodle-mation, as she calls it, lifts her black-polka-dot snout when she sees us, then stands and stretches lazily. A ribbon ties fluffy white hair atop the dog's head, and I know without looking that Babe's nails are painted. Purple, of course.

Before I turn off the ignition, Dottie opens her door and takes the box of éclairs from the seat. "Hey there, Babe." Her quiet little-girl giggle bubbles with delight.

Envy vibrates in my chest like a plucked guitar string, startling me with its clarity. I crave the joy I hear in her laughter, her sense of belonging, her natural acceptance of this place as a vital part of her soul. To her, this is home, not an embarrassing memory.

After letting the dogs out of the car, Dottie opens the gate and Hoot bounds through it, eager to check out Babe. His paws billow powder-fine dust into the air, making me cough. Saxon, though, hangs close to me, wary.

"Quiet, Hoot," Dottie hisses. "I want to sneak up on Aunt Maeve." She motions me forward.

Wind chimes hang from the mailbox by the door, their long silver cylinders jingling in the wind like sleigh bells. But it's the conversation drifting from the open kitchen window that takes me back. Back to junior high...a classmate and her mother dropping me off after working late together at school on a project...the woman's tight, superior smile when I opened the car door to the same laughter I hear now and my aunt's voice when it was much younger...

"Good God-a-mighty, Dottie, where'd you find that wig? If you're not the spittin' image of Mae West, I don't know who is."

Dottie prancing out onto the porch wearing a platinum blonde wig, wiggling her pudgy ten-year-old hips, orange Popsicle staining her mouth. *"Look at me, I'm Mae West."* Slipping a pair of sunglasses on. *"Now I'm Lana Turner."* Pursing her lips, blowing a kiss toward the car. *"Don't I look like a glamour-puss?"*

"You don't think that's Grady she's talking to, do you?" Dottie whispers, pulling my thoughts back into the present. "I'd be warped for life if we found them doing the nasty on the kitchen table."

A woman from inside the trailer whines, "It's not funny, Maeve. I look like Bozo."

"Only, minus the bald spot," Aunt Maeve booms in her full-throttled Texas twang, then shrieks with laughter.

I glance at Dottie and whisper, "Doesn't sound like Grady to me."

"You're the one who wanted a red curly perm, Raelene," Aunt Maeve continues.

"And what I got is an orange Brillo pad." The front door swings open and Aunt Maeve's customer—Raelene, I presume—steps out onto the porch.

"Slow down there, honey," Aunt Maeve bellows from behind her. "Where are you headed? You owe me forty bucks."

"If you think I'm paying for this mess, think again."
Raelene stomps down the porch steps.

Babe growls at the woman.

Hoot prances at her feet, yapping.

Raelene glares at the dogs then at us, murder in her
eyes.

I can't blame her for being upset. She does look like
Bozo without the bald spot. I wouldn't pay, either.

As Raelene reaches the gate, Aunt Maeve appears
in the doorway wearing a flowing purple-and-red
caftan, a yellow scarf twisted through her wild mass
of silver-threaded black hair. Less than five feet tall
and almost as wide, she flashes, sparkles and smolders
with kohl-smudged eyes and matching burgundy lips
and nails. The bangles on her arms glint in the
sunlight and jingle along with the wind chimes.

"Raelene Roach, you get your bony ass back here!"
she yells, oblivious to Dottie and me. Throwing back
her arm, she lets something small and brown fly from
the palm of her hand. It misses the woman's hair by
less than an inch, sails past Dottie and me and lands
in the yard. Aunt Maeve teeters then stumbles
backward from the effort of throwing it. She lands on
her bottom in the doorway, her feet extended out
across the metal porch, her mouth forming an O that
matches both of her widened eyes.

Dottie drops the box of éclairs and we both rush past a grumbling Raelene and up the steps to Aunt Maeve's side. We each take hold of a fleshy arm and pull her to her feet.

"Are you okay?" I ask.

Fanning our aunt's face with her free hand, Dottie says, "Jesus, don't faint on us. I don't know CPR."

Aunt Maeve appears bewildered as she glances from Dottie to me and back again. Then her eyes clear and she whoops with joy. "My girls. Together again on my doorstep. Thank the stars."

I look down when Saxon nudges my ankle. Between his jaws, he carries the thing Aunt Maeve threw at Raelene. He drops it at my feet, and I bend to scoop it up. It's square and flat and hard. "What's this?"

"I baked brownies for my clients this morning."

I frown. "You threw a brownie at that woman?"

"I know." She readjusts the scarf in her hair and sighs. "I'm ashamed of myself. I've lost my arm. Only last year I would have brought the old biddy to her knees."

Dottie grins. "That *was* a piss-poor shot, if I do say so."

Aunt Maeve winks at her and the two begin to cackle. "Cinnamon stick, it's good to know you're as spicy as ever." She hugs my sister then holds her at arm's length. "Look at you!" Rubbing a hand across

Dottie's stomach, Aunt Maeve closes her eyes. "It feels like a boy. We'll ask the leaves."

All three dogs lay on the linoleum kitchen floor in front of the door, sick from consuming the dozen éclairs we forgot to take out of the yard. Squeezed in between the two larger, older dogs, Hoot pops one in the nose with a paw every so often.

Wigs of all lengths, colors and cuts on plastic heads line every inch of counter space. Clusters of odd-size candles flicker on the table. Incense burns on the window ledge, its pungent mossy aroma blending in the air with perm solution fumes. A soft flute flutters from Aunt Maeve's old turntable. Outside on the porch, I hear the tinkling wind chimes.

From the cabinet over the sink, Aunt Maeve removes a plastic pitcher of tea with a lid on it. For as long as I can remember, she has kept it there, the tea she brews every morning. At night, before bed, she pours out whatever is left over.

"This is so cheesy." I blow my bangs off my forehead. "I didn't drive all the way here to take part in one of your voodoo experiments."

Aunt Maeve tsk-tsks as she carries the pitcher and a spoon to the table where Dottie and I sit staring at a foam cup atop a paper plate. "Lemon drop, you never change. Sweet one minute, sour the next." She tosses back her hair. "What's it going to be? You want to keep your husband or not?"

Dottie toes my shin under the table. Her narrowed eyes indicate I should humor our aunt.

Back in high school, my sister claimed she didn't believe in Aunt Maeve's tea leaf magic any more than I did. But I could sense her enthusiasm whenever a client gave permission for her to sit in on a reading as Aunt Maeve's apprentice. I think she *wanted* to believe in it; I think she still does.

Tapping my fingers on the place mat in front of me, I frown at Aunt Maeve and say, "If it makes you happy, I'll do it."

Aunt Maeve nods toward the foam cup. Her voice transforms, drops from a blaring foghorn to a soft, dramatic vibration. "Pick it up."

Mumbling under my breath, I lift the cup.

Dottie leans forward.

"Now, with your other hand," my aunt instructs in the same husky Kathleen Turner tone, "use the teaspoon to take some leaves from the bottom of the pitcher."

"I know, I know. I didn't live with you for a decade without learning the ritual." Despite my best efforts not to.

Dipping deep into the pitcher with the spoon, I lift out a few soggy grinds then transfer them into the cup, mumbling, "I feel like an idiot."

"Now the tea," Dottie says, sounding far-too-excited for a nonbeliever.

"*I know.*"

"*Okay.*" Her nostrils flare. "Don't bite my head off."

I spoon up some of the golden liquid, dribble a few drops into the cup on top of the grinds. Then, before they can recite the next steps, I swirl the tea around the cup clockwise. The leaves swirl faster and faster until, quickly, I turn the cup upside down on the paper plate. Tea leaks out from beneath the rim.

"Thump it," Aunt Maeve whispers.

I thump the bottom of the cup, then turn it right side up again.

Aunt Maeve takes the cup from me and looks into it, her eyes dark and serious.

Dottie leans even farther toward the center of the table.

Candle flames dance. Incense smolders. The room is so quiet I hear our mingled breathing.

Hoot yaps once. Babe growls. Saxon whimpers.

Laughter bubbles up in me. I cover my mouth, my shoulders shaking.

Aunt Maeve cuts her eyes my way before lifting the

cup closer to her face for a better view of the symbols she supposedly sees stuck on the sides, formed by the tea leaves. Seconds count off on the wall clock. *Tick... tick...tick.* Loud as a dripping faucet in a sleeping house at midnight.

"What do you see?" Dottie whispers.

"Shh. Quiet, girl."

I snicker again.

"The hawk," Aunt Maeve breathes. "He represents jealousy." Her gaze darts to mine. "He has a heart clutched between his jaws."

"A heart?" Dottie's eyes widen.

"Love and trust." Aunt Maeve tilts her head to the side and her dangling earrings sway. "Your jealousy is killing the love and trust in your marriage," she informs me.

She learned that much from our prior conversation. Still, I feel a strange flutter in my chest. "It's hot in here," I complain, eager to change the subject. "Why won't you let me buy you a new air conditioner for the window?"

"I'm not a charity case," my aunt booms, her mysterious tea-reader voice from only seconds ago gone. Her eyes return to the contents of the cup.

"But—"

"Shh! Both of you."

Dottie snorts and we jump like scolded schoolgirls.

Aunt Maeve's eyes snap like a whip. "Good God-a-mighty, how's a woman supposed to concentrate?"

When Dottie's toe nudges my shin again, the corner of my mouth twitches.

"There's a lamp on one side of the cup." Once again, Aunt Maeve sounds dreamy and mysterious. "The lamp shines on a snake that's draped through a triangle."

Dottie's shoulders start shaking, too.

Oblivious to her two snorting nieces, Aunt Maeve continues, "The snake represents your enemy, Dinah. The lamp on the side means secrets will be revealed, the triangle…something unexpected."

Sobering, Dottie wipes her eyes and whispers, "Dinah's enemy reveals a secret that's unexpected?" Her gaze locks with mine.

We stare at each other, and corny as the whole thing is, my breath catches.

"Track down that woman you saw with Stan. Talk to her," Aunt Maeve says. "You'll have your answers. But be prepared…they might surprise you."

I snatch the cup from her hand, crush it between my palms. "This is crazy. Those leaves don't mean anything."

Dottie exchanges a look with Aunt Maeve. "Quit

being so hardheaded, Di. Tracking down that hussy couldn't hurt. Who knows? It might help." She shrugs. "It beats staring at your computer and making a half-assed attempt to work."

I know she's right. I've spent a lifetime trying to avoid scenes and sidestep controversy. If confronting Lou Lou will lead me to the truth, then that's what I should do.

CHAPTER 8

We spend the night at Aunt Maeve's since Dottie's sleepy and I've had too much wine. All of our earlier talk about Stan and the other woman brought my uncertainties and fear to the surface again. But I also felt an odd sense of contentment, sitting alongside my sister in the trailer where we grew up, both of us snickering while our flaky aunt did her thing.

I never expected the three of us to be together again, a family gathered around the kitchen table. Not *The Brady Bunch* family I longed for in my youth. Not by a long shot. Still, reconnecting with the women who have shaped me the most quenched a thirst that I hadn't been aware I had. Today, I came face-to-face with my past and for once, didn't look away. It wasn't pretty, but it wasn't as ugly as the picture I'd painted in my mind. It didn't diminish me.

Now, as I try to go to sleep, I wonder if, like me, Dottie feels the strangeness of sharing this room again, this bed. The musty air sifting in through the window carries memories. Crickets chirp gossip about long-past scandals and old heartaches. On the railroad tracks behind the trailer park, the midnight train passes through town and, sensing my mood, lets loose a sorrowful wail.

I stare at the curve of my sister's shoulder, silhouetted in the darkness by the light of the moon. The first couple of years after we moved in with Aunt Maeve, Dottie was my security, my soul mate. She was the one person in the world who, like me, understood the bewilderment and self-doubt of awakening one morning to discover that your mother had packed up and disappeared in the night.

When Patsy Dewberry took off to chase her silver-screen dreams, she left behind the things no longer of use to her: old terry-cloth house shoes with holes in the toes, a sliver of honeysuckle-scented soap at the edge of the bathtub, her gardening gloves. And us.

Only Dottie knew the panic of watching the back of your father's car vanish at the end of the road after he dropped you off in a strange place. Left you to live with a wild-looking woman he said was his sister, but whom you had never seen before.

As long as I had Dottie beside me, I had a link to my parents and the life I remembered, the family that had not been perfect, but that was familiar. And mine.

But time passed and the bewilderment, self-doubt and panic morphed into anger. I no longer wanted a link to the parents who betrayed me, whom I had trusted to protect me at all costs. The people who should have loved me most had failed me most. Dottie was a reminder of that. I resented her for it, and for becoming my responsibility. Just as she resented me for being the "good" sister. The one who always did everything right.

A breeze ripples the purple velvet curtain over the window, and my mind drifts back to another night, lying next to Dottie in this room when a different wind-ruffled curtain hung there, a red satin one.

I told her about the house of a classmate I had visited after school that day, about the crystal chandelier in the entry hall, the fancy Chinese rugs, the smell of lemon polish on the antique furniture that filled every room. I hummed the piano music that had played on the stereo while we studied in the kitchen. Described the balanced dinner the girl's mother had prepared for her daughter and husband, straight off the food pyramid chart from health class. Even now, I can hear my own voice whispering into the perm-scented darkness...

"And when Kim's dad came home from work? He kissed her mother on the cheek and gave her a hug. Mrs. Tyler's a real lady."

"Did she remind you of Mama?"

"Mama didn't cook. She's not a lady, either. That's for sure."

"That's okay, 'cause she's a star. Like Marilyn Monroe."

"When did you ever see Mama in a movie?"

"Maybe we just don't recognize her anymore. Maybe she changed her name. That's what I'll probably do when I go to Hollywood."

"You'll never go to Hollywood. And Mama isn't a star. She only liked to pretend, like you in your stupid wigs and sunglasses."

"At least I don't worry all the time about what people think."

"Shut up. I don't worry."

"Uh-huh. You're always embarrassed. You want us to be boring just like everybody else."

That night, I tied off a piece of my heart. If I stood apart from my parents' memory, from my sister and even Aunt Maeve, I could make believe that, long ago, I had lived a life like my classmate's. Calm and simple and uncluttered. Secure and stable. With two respectable parents who loved each other and put us first, Dottie and me.

A life admired, instead of whispered and laughed about, by everybody in town.

* * *

When I drag myself from bed the next morning, Dottie is at the kitchen table flipping through old picture albums. Aunt Maeve stands at the counter toasting Pop-Tarts and smothering them with butter—her idea of a balanced breakfast.

"'Mornin', lemon drop."

I yawn. "Good morning."

Dottie glances up and says, "Hey."

"Where're the dogs?"

"Outside having their breakfast." Aunt Maeve nods toward the refrigerator. "There's a pitcher of Tang made."

I take it out, get three glasses from the cupboard.

Aunt Maeve carries a paper plate piled high with Pop-Tarts to the table, grabs a roll of paper towels, then we sit down.

"Who is this?" Dottie taps her fingernail against a photograph. "I've seen it before, but I can't remember."

Aunt Maeve leans over to look. "That's me and your mama. We couldn't have been more than twelve." Blurting a laugh, she shakes her head. "You looked just like her at that age, Dot. You're like her in other ways, too. We were best friends, you know. All through school. What a pair we made. That Patsy was the sassiest little flirt. My brother was a goner the minute he laid eyes on her after she moved to Coopersville in third grade."

My mind slams shut. I don't want to hear the same old stories about my parents I've suffered through all my life. I don't care about their history. Dottie remembers the tales, too, though she pretends she doesn't. Why does she torture herself?

Dottie flips the page with a wistful smile. "How old was Daddy?"

"Three years older than Patsy and me. But he followed her around like a puppy dog." Taking a bite of Pop-Tart, Aunt Maeve shakes her head over a different shot of my parents together. "That was taken shortly before they married. Look at that heart-breaking face. She knew how to use it, too. Your mama could be selfish. And helpless in a lot of ways. Oh, she meant well. Patsy always had good intentions, she just never grew up. She craved excitement like I crave sugar. Al was so love struck he didn't care a whit, though." She nods at the picture and adds, "Not then, anyway."

Against my will, I'm drawn to the photo, to the face so like Dottie's. Memories flood my mind, bringing with them an ache that fills every cell of my body. The stroke of Mama's hands in my hair as she braided it, a voice smooth as velvet humming "My Funny Valentine."

Comfort and false promises after I'd had a bad dream. *"I'm here, baby. I'm right here beside you for always."*

My attention shifts to my father, dark and reed thin. Strong shoulders and muscled arms I thought would carry me wherever he went.

How can Dottie still obsess about parents whose actions sent her searching for love in the backseats of too many cars, for acceptance in the bottom of too many bottles? Why does Aunt Maeve nurture that obsession? Since we were girls, our aunt always claimed Dottie was like our mother, not seeming to realize the implications of that statement.

"I'm surprised your fingerprints aren't engraved on to the pages of that album, you looked at it so much growing up," I say, hating my harsh tone, but unable to subdue it. I grab a Pop-Tart and snap off a piece. "How many times do you have to see those pictures and hear those same old stories?"

Ignoring me, Dottie asks, "Why did we move out of Coopersville after I was born?"

"Al got a job out in Southern California," Aunt Maeve says. "That's where Patsy really caught the acting bug. Oh, she'd always dreamed of being a star, but I don't think she took it serious until y'all moved out there."

"Why do you think she married Daddy if she

wanted to act? Why didn't she just pack up and go to Hollywood when she graduated high school?"

Aunt Maeve studies me with knowing eyes then says to Dottie, "I think it was just something she did in the heat of the moment without thinking it through. Patsy would get an idea in her head and she'd do it." She breaks another Pop-Tart in half. "You know how it is, honey." Her tone seems to say, *you've done your share of the same.*

Dottie closes the album, picks up her glass of juice, then sets it down and stares into it, quiet now, a troubled look in her eyes.

Why can't she let it go? Forget our parents and move on? For all we know, our mother's dead by now. Sometimes, I hope she is. Others, I yearn to feel her hands stroke my hair again, to smell her honeysuckle scent, to hear her crystal voice singing all the songs she loved, just one more time.

"Patsy was crazy about you two girls," my aunt says, when the silence stretches too long. "From the minute you were born. She loved dressing you up and playing with you. She called you her little dolls."

My laugh holds no humor. "*Paper* dolls. That's what we were to her. Pretty and disposable." Mama dressed us up, played with us, then threw us away when she became bored.

* * *

Dottie is uncharacteristically quiet on the drive home.

"What's the matter?" I finally ask.

"Before you got up this morning, Aunt Maeve told me Daddy called a couple of weeks back."

I grip the steering wheel tighter. "Why didn't she tell me?"

"She knew you wouldn't want to talk about him."

"She's right."

Her foot taps against the floorboard. Faster. Faster. "He may come for the Fourth of July."

"Then I'll be watching fireworks somewhere else."

Silence, then, "Maybe we should see him."

The thought of facing him again shoots panic through me. I tell myself I don't care what he thinks. Yet, I can't bear the idea of him learning my marriage is failing, as his marriage failed. I don't want him to know that Stan left me, like Mama left him. I don't want him thinking that we have anything in common.

Doesn't Dottie feel the same? Doesn't she care that he would find out she's pregnant and giving up her child, like he and Mama gave us up?

We're better than they were, Dottie and I. That's what I want him to know. They didn't hurt us. We didn't need them. But he might look at our lives and think otherwise. "Why should we see him?" I ask.

"I don't know. He's been on my mind. Mama, too." I glance across at Dottie, see her settle a hand on her stomach. "I want some questions answered. About both of them. I'm tired of being a chicken shit. I'm ready to just look him in the eye and ask."

"You're not the chicken shit, Dottie. He is. That man doesn't deserve one millisecond of your attention."

Beneath her tan, her skin flushes pink as she turns to look out the window. "I've done some dumb-ass things. This baby's living proof of that. But one thing I've learned is that, if you want to know something, you won't find out by sitting back and twiddling your thumbs."

What is it about her at this moment that drops my heart in slow motion to the pit of my stomach? The look on her face, the stroke of her fingertips against the protrusion beneath her T-shirt. I sense a vulnerability I've rarely seen in Dottie before.

Daddy dumping us with Aunt Maeve hurt Dottie; I know that. But she's never been as bitter over it as me. I'll never understand why. The last time he dropped into our lives was my high school graduation. Dottie, fifteen at the time, had an instant personality change. She acted giddy over his arrival, adoringly shy. She soaked up his honeyed compliments like a brand-new sponge. *Look at my girls…all grown up and pretty as rose petals.*

He said he was planning to stay and look for a job, but I didn't buy it. I refused the graduation gift that he tried to give me, a tiny box wrapped up in wrinkled paper and topped with a cheap stick-on bow. The shine in Al Dewberry's eyes dulled like a tarnished rhinestone after my rejection of his offering. I couldn't have cared less. At that moment, I knew that I never wanted to see him again, that he wasn't worth spitting on.

After the ceremony, he said he'd meet us back at the trailer for cake, but he never showed up. When he left the school auditorium, he also left Coopersville. Our lives. He never came back. He never called, and only wrote once, right after. *Something came up, and I had to leave. I promise I'll be back soon, girls. Quick as a whistle.*

Two years later, at Dottie's graduation, she scanned the bleachers with a hopeful expression, and I suffered a twinge of guilt that my coldness toward him last time might have kept him away. But Dottie was better off without him there. Our father's lies were like a drug to her, seductive and poisonous; his presence would have only given her false hope.

"Aren't you ready to put all the crap behind you?" Dottie asks quietly.

"I *have* put it behind me."

She huffs. "Who do you think you're talking to? Until you make your peace with them, they'll always be like a bad dream you can't wake up from."

"You think our father can change anything now? What's done is done. He can't take it back."

"No, but we can dump everything on the table and sort through it. Find closure. That's what the shrinks call it. They say it's important."

"Do you see a therapist?"

"No, but I watch *Dr. Phil*."

I'm not sure why, but that makes me smile. I imagine my sister on his show, spilling her guts, him trying to figure her out. I imagine Dr. Phil in her face, telling her what's what in a stern voice, Aunt Maeve running in and handing her a brownie, Dottie aiming at his forehead, raring back and scoring a bull's eye. I start to laugh.

Dottie scowls at me. "What?"

"Nothing, just—you on *Dr. Phil*. What a show that would be."

She tilts her head to one side and studies me. "What's got into you? You've changed. The way you were with Aunt Maeve yesterday. With me."

I shrug. "People grow up."

"Not all people."

She's right. According to Aunt Maeve, our mother didn't. Yesterday I would have said Dottie never did, either, and never will. Today, I'm not so sure.

After we arrive home, I make lunch. We eat, then Dottie naps. I call my attorney and make an appointment for next week, then work on my article. While I write, Dottie is never off my mind. Her vulnerability during the drive back from Coopersville. The way she cradled her swollen stomach. Her need to come to terms with family disappointments, to acquire information from our father that might help her repair her damaged heart.

Is she changing her mind about giving me the baby? Is she trying to get her life on track so that she can trust herself to be a good mother? If so, I should be relieved. What if Stan doesn't come back? What if I'm as insignificant to him as the clothing he's yet to pick up? Would it be wise to try and raise the baby without him?

Dottie is full of energy when she wakes up, so we go shopping for maternity clothes. As we carry sacks from the department store to the car, she grumbles about looking like a sexless frump in the jeans she wears out of the mall, instead of the ones she arrived in. They have a stretchy front panel for her pooch and an elastic waist. Frumpy or not, she looks a hundred times more comfortable, and I think to myself that the baby must be breathing easier, too.

When I ask if she's up for looking at baby clothes, she says she's charred on shopping and, anyway, she'd leave that for me to do. I take this as reassurance that she hasn't changed her mind about the baby, after all. She's unaffected by tiny booties and gowns, by fluffy, rabbit-soft blankets. Those small things that excite me, don't interest her at all. At least that's what I tell myself.

We stop for frozen yogurt on the way home at an ice-cream parlor and sit at an outdoor table.

I spoon a bite and watch her. "I need to ask you some things about the baby's father."

"He's not important." She licks her cone.

"He is important. My lawyer said we'd need to have him sign papers relinquishing his rights."

"Put them in the mail. I'll give you his address. I'd rather wear maternity clothes for the rest of my life than see that bastard again."

"We'll ask the attorney next week if we can mail them. You might have to call the father, though." I twirl my plastic spoon in the creamy chocolate vanilla swirl. "Does he know you're pregnant?"

Her brows rise, but she keeps her eyes on the cone.

"He knows. He won't give a rat's ass about the adoption. He needs a kid even less than I do."

I can see that she's uncomfortable talking about him. Still, I take a deep breath and ask, "Who is he?"

"Just some lousy lounge lizard who makes love even worse than he plays piano." She sighs. "His name is Dave Reno."

"Did he work at the same casino you did?"

"The same hotel. In one of the bars."

"Did you love him?"

"Jesus." Dottie winces. "Give me some credit for having at least a *little* class."

I cross my arms and lean back, frustrated with her. "Well, you slept with the guy, Dottie."

"Don't rub it in." Shaking her head, she mutters, "One time. Him and his cheap off-brand rubbers." With a glance at her stomach, she adds, "If this doesn't teach me to lay off the martinis, nothing will."

We finish our yogurt in silence. Cars pass by on the street. Sunshine seeps into my pores. The heat feels so good, I convince myself the benefits of the vitamin D outweigh the threat of skin cancer. "Will you see Dave again when you go back to Vegas after the baby's born?" I ask.

"I'm not going back."

Stan's prediction that she is stringing me along stabs

into my thoughts, and I'm suddenly afraid. "Where will you go?" Before she can answer, I take a steadying breath then ask, "Or do you plan to stay here?"

"I don't know. I haven't decided."

After our visit to Aunt Maeve's, I had thought we were making progress, coming closer to one another, sharing our feelings more openly. But, at this moment, much more than a table separates me from my sister.

Four in the morning and still no sleep. I turn on my nightstand lamp, jerk the covers aside and climb from bed. Saxon lifts his head from Stan's pillow and stares at me with half-open eyes.

"Go back to sleep," I whisper.

He blinks a couple of times, moans, then lowers his head again.

I make my way through the house to my office without turning on lights. I don't want to wake Dottie and have her see me like this; my face swollen from hours of crying, my nose raw from blowing it into a half box of tissues.

When we arrived home from shopping this evening, Stan's things were gone from the house. Oh, not all of them, no. And that provides the hope that I cling to as tightly as the Silver Lace vine clings to the chain-link fence around Aunt Maeve's yard.

Pitiful, that's me. Thinking he'll find he can't survive without those clothes he left hanging on his side of the closet. The sweater collection his mom adds to each Christmas, the ones he only wears when she visits. The worn-out slacks, out-of-style shirts and too-wide ties he should've taken to Goodwill years ago. He'll need them, I tell myself. He'll come back for them. And when he does, he'll realize that he needs me, too.

But, in my heart, I know that isn't true. He left behind the clothes he no longer wanted. The ones worn-out, out of style or outgrown.

Has he outgrown me, too?

I close the door to my office, then turn on the light while Dottie's words echo through my mind. *If you want to know something, you won't find out by sitting back and twiddling your thumbs.*

Maybe her mistakes have taught her some things about living, things I could stand to learn, as well.

Sitting in my desk chair, I face the computer and turn it on. Music blares from the speakers. I lower the volume. The glow of the screen seems too bright, spotlighting my crime.

Wrong. This is just wrong, plain and simple. Tapping into someone else's e-mail. Even if that someone is my cheating husband. But how else will I get my answers when he won't talk to me? And following the rules, behaving myself has gotten me nowhere. At least the last time I read Stan's messages, I learned something. It may have been painful, but it brought me a step closer to the truth. It's time to take the next step now.

I type in his user name and password. His mailbox appears on the screen. And there it is…another message from Lou Lou, dated tonight—or, I should say, this morning—and already opened.

I click on it and, as I read, outrage erupts inside of me. Hot, sharp and searing.

Stan,
Sorry we were interrupted. You were great, by the way. If you need to get in touch with me before tomorrow night, call my cell phone. I forgot to tell you I've changed the number. It's 555-4048.
Lou Lou

You were great. Now I understand how otherwise model citizens can commit murder when blinded by fury so strong it obliterates rationality. If Lou Lou were here right now, I'd strangle her. Stan, too.

Trembling, I click into Stan's saved messages file and find his message back to Lou Lou, sent only an hour ago.

Hey,
I need to see you before tomorrow night. Can you
stop by the station in the morning around ten? If
anyone asks, you came to pay a traffic ticket.
Stan

The screen blurs in front of my eyes. He lets her
come to the station? Do his co-workers know about
the affair? His new partner, Will? Does Pete? Not one
to mix his personal life with business, Stan never liked
me to come to the station unless it was absolutely
necessary.

Suddenly, I hear Aunt Maeve as clearly as if she's
in the room...

*The snake represents your enemy, Dinah. The lamp on
the side means secrets will be revealed, the triangle...some-
thing unexpected.*

Ten o'clock in the morning.

A bus station sits catty-corner from the police
station, across the street. At no later than nine forty-
five, I'll be sitting on the bench, watching the door for
Lou Lou.

The snake.

CHAPTER 9

The next morning at nine-thirty, Dottie and I pull into a parking space two blocks from the police station. After turning off the ignition, I check my reflection in the rearview mirror. With any luck, the cap and sunglasses disguise me enough that Stan won't recognize me should he glance out a window toward the bus station. I'll only be another person waiting for a ride.

"Let's go," I say to Dottie.

Yawning, she rubs her eyes. "No way am I sitting outside in this wind. We can see the door from here."

As if on cue, a strong gale hits the car, rocking it slightly. "I don't want to take any chances on missing her."

"A woman like that? I could spot her a mile away. You should be more worried about Stanny spotting you. Disguised or not, you're his wife, and he's a cop. He's trained to notice suspicious-looking people."

"I look suspicious?"

"I bet pretty much the same people wait on the ten o'clock bus every day, don't you?"

Wind whistles at the windows. The air outside is hazy with dust; it sneaks in through the air vents making me sneeze. "Maybe you're right."

For five minutes, we sit in silence while Dottie files her nails, chews gum and curses the weather. In spite of her bad attitude, I'm thankful she came along. Today, more than ever, I need someone beside me.

Fidgeting, I watch the station's entrance. Why would Stan want his mistress to come here? As a precaution? That must be it. He could tell anyone who asked that she was there with information about a case, or to file a complaint, or any other number of reasons. But a friend or acquaintance might say something to me if they saw him keeping company outside of work with a beautiful woman like Lou Lou.

From my purse, I retrieve the envelope of photographs that we picked up at the drugstore earlier, the ones Dottie took of Stan and Lou Lou standing outside of Wong's, as well as a few accidents that snapped when the car salesman startled us: one of the dashboard, another of my elbow, an extremely unflattering close-up of Wayne's left nostril. But Dottie captured some good shots of Stan and Lou Lou with the zoom. Although she wears too much makeup,

Stan's other woman is a curvaceous goddess. A modern-day Venus.

I glance from the photos to the station entrance and back again. Still no Lou Lou.

In the picture I hold, Stan wears sunglasses. He looks a bit stiff and uneasy. More than likely, he feared being seen by someone he knows. Which he should've been, since that's exactly what happened.

When I look up, the station doors swing open. I sit forward, but relax again when two uniformed officers exit the building. They cross the street, headed for the parking lot.

Returning my attention to the photographs, I flip to the next one. Lou Lou is animated as she leans toward Stan, the umbrella tilted to reveal her face, her free hand lifted in front of her. I study her expression and rage whips through me like the wind outside whips the police station flags. I want to rip the photo to shreds, break something. I want to scream until my vocal cords bleed. How could I have been so stupid to think he was faithful to me when he was really sleeping with another woman? Is that what Lou Lou is smiling about in the picture? My naiveté? How clever they've been to fool me? Behind his dark glasses, is Stan smiling, too? Or does he not think of me at all when they're together? Am I the last thing on his mind? Not worth the effort of worrying over?

Trembling, I return the photographs to my purse. "I can't stand this waiting. I might as well walk down to the bus stop. I'll take a chance on Stan seeing me."

Dottie shrugs. "Hang on to your hat."

Waiting on the bench is worse than waiting in the car. Squeezed between an old woman in a knitted stocking hat and a young man with hair so greasy the wind doesn't budge it, I watch the street for signs of Lou Lou. And fret. Will she be on the Harley today or in a vehicle? Will she "dress up" for Stan again? Wear something that shows off those mile-long legs to perfection? Will he take her somewhere private under the guise of questioning her? Or maybe he doesn't need a pretense at work. Maybe I'm the only one in his circle he's kept in the dark about the affair. The clueless wife. A fool.

On my left, the greasy-haired man gapes at me with dull, vacant eyes. He smells sour, like dried, three-day-old sweat. The frail, elderly woman hacks out one cough after another without covering her mouth. I'm relieved when the city transit arrives, my bench mates get on and the bus pulls away, belching exhaust.

Down the block, a car horn blares. Dottie waves to capture my attention. She points to the red motorcycle, and my heart slams against my chest when it pulls to the curb across the street. The rider climbs off, then removes a big white helmet. And there it is…that sleek blond hair. Lou Lou. No doubt about it. Same size, same cycle, same pink shoes.

Jealousy throbs at my temples. Her hair may be great, but her clothes are better. A crisp summery ensemble. From the lime-sherbet-colored jacket that I would swear is cashmere, to the full legs of the white slacks, all the way down to the pale pink shoes that I have a sinking feeling aren't cheap knockoffs as I'd hoped, but the real thing. High-dollar designers Carrie on *Sex and the City* would be proud to prance around town in.

I stand, agape, as Lou Lou glides through the station's front door and disappears and, though I recognize the sound of my Honda Accord's horn honking, several seconds pass before I glance in that direction. Dottie waves me over, but I ignore her.

The next twenty minutes are spent pacing in front of the bench, too caught up in painful, heart-wrenching confusion and in plotting revenge to be bothered by the wind.

An incident I never thought twice about when it occurred comes back to haunt me. On our last anniversary, Stan took me to brunch at an upscale café, not knowing that a local boutique for plus-size women was hosting a fashion show there. Before the waitress seated us, I suggested we go somewhere else, but Stan thought it might be fun to stay and watch. He enjoyed himself, ogling the voluptuous, full-figured models with an appreciative twinkle in his eye.

Is that the problem? Does he feel shortchanged by my less than curvaceous figure?

I scoff at myself. People don't start extramarital affairs because they want a more physically desirable partner; they start them because they're insecure in the marriage, because they feel something is missing. Or maybe they just need an ego boost.

Okay, I admit it. Sometimes I watch *Dr. Phil*, too.

The night of my birthday, when Stan and I had argued, he'd accused me of being obsessed with having a baby, of letting it take over our lives. Is that true? Did I become so preoccupied with my need to conceive that I ignored *Stan's* needs? His emotional ones? When was the last time we really had fun together? Laughed until we cried? When was the last time I made love to my husband just because I wanted *him*, not because I was trying to make a baby?

By the time Lou Lou pushes through the station doors again and heads to her cycle, my feet hurt from pacing. I hurry down the block toward the car. Dottie, in the driver's seat now, meets me halfway. The car screeches to a stop beside me as Lou Lou eases toward the intersection.

I run to the passenger door of the Accord. Glancing over my shoulder, I see the traffic light turn red and the cycle halt.

Dottie rolls down the window and yells, "Get in!"

Panting from exertion, weather-beaten, my ego even more battered and bruised than before, I slump in the seat beside her and cross my arms.

"It's about time," Dottie says. "My butt's numb from all that sitting." She pulls to the light, stopping directly behind the cycle. "Who wears white pants on a Harley? And those shoulders…she looks like a line-backer for the Dallas Cowboys."

I'm sure her exaggerations are meant to console me, but they don't work. I scowl at the back of Lou Lou's head and fume. At myself, mostly. There's no good excuse for an affair, but maybe I did push Stan away.

"Well?" Dottie looks across at me. "Say something."

"What do you want me to say?"

"Talk trash about her. It'll make you feel better."

"I doubt it. Besides, I'd only be lying. She's a great dresser, she's poised and she's obviously comfortable in her body."

Dottie pulls a pack of cigarettes and a lighter from

her purse, smirking at me when she sees my disapproving expression. "I don't get it. You aren't pissed at that woman for screwing your husband, but you are at me for this?" Shaking a cigarette free from the pack, she says, "Don't worry. I'm only going to light it and *smell* the tobacco."

"Haven't you ever heard of secondhand smoke?" I bite back a lecture as she flicks the lighter until it flames, then holds it to the cigarette's tip.

The traffic light turns green. Inhaling deeply, Dottie follows Lou Lou through the intersection. She props the hand holding the burning cigarette on her thigh so that the smoke curls up toward her face.

Menthol laces the air. I keep my focus on the cycle ahead as we take the Interstate all the way to the city's southwest side. When Lou Lou exits, Dottie does, too. We follow the motorcycle into a strip of shops that line the road alongside the shopping mall. Lou Lou parks in front of Nails by Nona, and we pull in beside her. She climbs from the cycle and enters the shop.

"Oh, good," Dottie says, turning off the ignition then looking at her nails. "I could use a manicure. A pedicure, too." She glances across at me. "That is, if you're buying."

"You could've had Aunt Maeve paint them for free."

"I didn't want her to spend our whole visit working."

I take a deep breath to steady my nerves, then shake my head. "I can't go in there."

"Sure you can. Don't you let that floozy intimidate you."

I *am* intimidated. By Lou Lou's looks. Her size. The regal way she carries herself. Most of all, I'm intimidated by the hold she has on my husband. Her ability to distract him from our marriage, his work. The two things that once meant everything to him.

Stubbing out the cigarette butt in the ashtray, Dottie says, "You can do this."

I meet her gaze, and think what a riddle she has become in seventeen years. When we were young, I knew what to expect of her. Always. How she would react in any situation. Now she constantly surprises me. One minute she's an older version of her previous tough self, the next she softens around the edges.

Taking a deep breath, I reach for the door handle. "Okay. Let's go."

Outside Nona's, Dottie pauses. "Ready?"

"What should I say to her?"

"Wing it." Her grin is mischievous. "Why don't you let me start off doing the talking? You just hang back and get a good look at the woman…imagine her together with Stanny. Then, when you finally get pissed enough, feel free to jump right in."

Several minutes later, Dottie and I sit in pedicure chairs on either side of Lou Lou, our feet submerged in bubbling warm water. The nail technician rubs sloughing salts into one of Lou Lou's heels. Lou Lou's eyes are closed, and her massive breasts jiggle as the chair's massage mechanism pummels her back.

My gaze lingers on her face, and my heart pumps so hard and fast I'm dizzy. Her bone structure is flawless. High cheekbones, nice chin, delicate brow and jawline. Why would she wear all that makeup? Maybe, beneath it, her skin is bad. I find myself hoping that's the case. That her cheeks are acne-scarred, her forehead dotted with an ugly brown age spot or two.

"Ahh. Fabulous." Lou Lou's eyes flutter open and she catches me watching her. She smiles, and I feel my face flush as I quickly look away. All I can think about is the fact that her eyes are the soft blue of a summer sky and exotic, that her teeth are pearl-white, straight, dazzling.

The guilt I had earlier over not meeting Stan's emotional needs evaporates along with the steam rising from the water. No wonder Stan wants her. She's mesmerizing, intriguing in her self-confidence.

Any other woman so tall, with such broad shoulders might slump. Not her. And she doesn't try to disguise her long feet with bland, boring shoes. She carries herself with dignity, even flaunts her size. Lou Lou likes the way she looks, and the result is irresistible.

I'd admire her if I didn't hate her so much.

"Lift, please," says the tiny Asian woman sitting on a stool at my feet. I raise my left foot from the water, prop it on a stand. She dries it with a towel, then goes to work on my calluses with a pumice stone.

"Excuse me," Dottie says to Lou Lou, as her own pedicure proceeds. "How did you turn that on?"

"The chair?" Her voice is Lauren Bacall husky, as intriguing as the rest of her.

Tapping a hand against the chair's arm, Lou Lou says, "This little lever here? One twist." She winks. "It will take you straight to heaven."

Dottie twists the lever and her chair purrs to life. Her upper body starts jiggling in perfect synchrony with Lou Lou's. "Thanks." Her eyelids flutter. "God, that's better than sex. And a lot less dangerous." Patting her stomach, she smiles. "You on your lunch hour?"

"No, I work nights. I own a club called The Pink Slipper."

I glance down at the sharp-toed pink shoes beside her chair.

"The Pink Slipper, huh? Never heard of it," Dottie says. "'Course, I haven't been back in town long." She looks across at me. "You heard of that club?"

I shake my head, afraid of what might exit my mouth if I open it. Good thing Dottie didn't call me by name, in case Stan talks to Lou Lou about me. Or does she even know he's married? She must, or why would they be sneaking around?

Reaching for her purse on the floor, Lou Lou says, "We opened four months ago. Here. Let me give you my business card." She retrieves two cards, hands one to Dottie and one to me. "Stop in some time. Those are good for a free drink."

Nodding and forcing a smile, I reach to a side table and pick up a magazine.

Dottie says, "Thanks," then adds, "I've waited my share of tables. Tended bar, too. You wouldn't be hiring, would you? I could sure use a job."

A peculiar smile creeps over Lou Lou's face. "Wish I could help you, sweetie, but I'm afraid you wouldn't fit in with the rest of the staff."

"Why? Haven't you ever had a pregnant waitress before?"

She sputters a laugh. "That would be one for the history books. For the medical textbooks, too."

Dottie looks as baffled as I am by that statement.

"The Pink Slipper just isn't your kind of place, sweetie," Stan's hussy adds.

"Are you kidding?" Dottie scoffs. "I've worked all kinds. Nothing much shocks me. My butt's been pinched, slapped and kissed so many times, I've lost count."

Lou Lou throws her head back and laughs. "It's not like that." In one quick movement, she grabs hold of the top of her hair, lifts it. A *wig*. Underneath, is a scalp as smooth and glossy as a boiled egg.

All the air leaves my lungs in a rush. My mind refuses to register what my eyes see. My ears ring. My vision blurs. It's as if I'm looking at Lou Lou through water, a murky sea of denial that distorts her image into a grotesque caricature.

"What I mean, sweetie," Lou Lou says to Dottie, "is you don't meet the requirements. No offense."

My pulse shoots up, pulling me with it to the surface. Lou Lou. *Lou Lou? Not* as in Louise? As in *Louis?* Oh my God. *Oh my God!* Stan is—no. *No.* The magazine slips through my fingers, hits my lap then drops to the floor. Flustered, I sit forward, look down at it and catch sight of Lou Lou's foot in the Asian woman's hands. Dark hair dusts the top of each toe.

The tiny woman looks up, points at the big toe, chirps, "You need wax?"

"About three days ago from the looks of it," Lou Lou answers with a chortle, replacing the wig and lifting the opposite foot from the water for a look. Sighing, she smiles at Dottie. "What we do for the sake of femininity."

Dottie makes a weak attempt to hide her shock. "It's the pits, isn't it?"

They laugh, then Lou Lou's eyes close again.

With one of her hands covering her mouth, Dottie widens *her* eyes at me until they bulge.

Returning my attention to Lou Lou, I think of everything I've envied about her, all the assets she has to offer Stan that I don't. A flawless face. Fashion sense. Big boobs. A sense of adventure.

My gaze skims lower, to the space between her hip bones…and one more thing Lou Lou has to offer that I'm missing.

Dottie drives since I'm too upset. "He's good," she says. "I'm no stranger to drag queens. Vegas is full of them. But he had me fooled."

I keep my eyes closed, my head back against the seat. I want to tell her I'm not ready to discuss Lou Lou, but I'm too numb to speak.

"You may not want to hear this," Dottie continues, "but here's how I see it. You're looking at three possibilities. A—there's another woman, we just haven't found her yet."

Another double D in Stan's life besides Lou Lou? A female? The true owner of the bra? Believe it or not, I'm relieved by that possibility. An hour ago, I thought another woman was the worst obstacle I could face in my marriage. Now I know better. Worse things exist, but they're unfathomable. At least for me. I cringe and kick them aside each time they enter my mind.

Dottie, it seems, doesn't share my denial. "B," she

continues. "Lou Lou *is* the other woman. Which means, Stanny is gay."

I press my palms against my ears to block out the sound of her voice. "You're right. Not only do I not want to hear that, I *won't*." Stan having an affair is not completely out of the realm of my imagination. But Stan having an affair with a cross-dresser is. Lou Lou can't be the bra's owner. I refuse to even consider that as a possibility.

Keeping her gaze on the road, Dottie pulls my left hand away from the side of my head. "After what we just saw in there, I thought you'd be shockproof."

"I'm not shocked. I just don't believe it."

She changes lanes. "Wives find out their husbands are gay all the time, Dinah."

"Not me."

"Why? Because Stanny's Mr. Macho?"

"I've been married to the man five years and dated him for a year before that. I know what he likes. He likes women."

"Maybe he's bisexual," she says, point-blank.

I open my eyes and glare at her. "Could we move on to C, please?"

"Whatever you say. I doubt B is the right answer, anyhow." Stopping at a red light, she inhales noisily, exhales and says, "C—Stan's not having an affair. The bra is his. *He* wears it."

"Nope." My stomach churns. My pulse flutters like a leaf in a tornado. C is no better than B. And just as impossible. "Not a chance."

"So, what? You're gonna act like none of this ever happened? That'll only make things worse."

"Please. No more Phil-analysis. Okay?"

The light changes, and Dottie steps on the gas. "Pretending the answer is 'none of the above' won't get you anywhere. Since you won't even listen to B or C, do you think it's A? That there's another woman?"

I nod.

"You act like you want it to be that. Which I guess I might, too, if I were you. I mean, competing with a female is one thing, but a man?" She makes a scoffing sound. "Even I wouldn't know where to start. But surely you wouldn't rather him have a woman on the side than be wearing that bra, would you?" When I don't respond, she repeats, "*Would* you?"

Chewing the inside of my cheek, I nod again.

Dottie barks a laugh. "You'd rather your husband be sleeping with another woman than wearing women's underwear? Haven't you been kicked around enough in your life?"

I wonder if she refers to our abandonment, what she did to me in Austin seventeen years ago, or both?

"Stan screwing around is cheating, Dinah. Stan wearing a lacy bra under his flap jacket and Victoria's Secret panties below his gun belt isn't." She giggles, then cuts it short.

"You'd like that, wouldn't you? Nothing would make you happier than to find out Stan is a cross-dresser. You've had it in for him since the moment the two of you met."

She pulls the car into the alley that runs behind my house. "*Me?* I think you've got that backward."

"You can't stand for me to have a normal, healthy, meaningful relationship with a man. You know why? Because *you* don't have one. You never have and you never will. You're too immature to care about anybody but yourself. Even your baby."

Dottie's face flushes crimson. "You're sad, Dinah, you know that? You're so hung up on normal it's pathetic. Well, guess what? The joke's on you. Seems the guy you chose to marry isn't any more *normal* than the family you turned your back on."

Stung, I take deep breaths. Maybe I deserved that. Maybe my words were too harsh, too hurtful, and she's on the defensive. But, right now, I can't find it in my heart to be sorry. Her eagerness to turn Stan into something he isn't, something that would, in all likelihood, ruin our marriage, grates on me.

Dottie turns into my driveway. Pressing her lips into a thin line, she pushes the button hooked over the visor. The garage door rises. "I understand you're upset," she says quietly. "You want to tear into somebody, and I'm handy. Let her rip. I'm used to it."

I stare out the side window, hating this day, hating the fact that my sister and I can't seem to stop hurting each other, hating the uncertainties racing through my mind about Stan.

When the garage door lowers behind us and she turns off the engine, I climb out. "There's another woman," I say. "That's the only answer."

Dottie slams her door and follows me into the house. "No it's not," she says bluntly. "It's the *least likely* answer."

I let the dogs in from the backyard, and Hoot almost knocks me over in his exuberance. Saxon whimpers when I don't give him more than a pat on the head before heading for the living room. "Why can't you just drop it?" I ask Dottie as we both collapse on the couch.

"Because, if I'm right, your marriage isn't in as much trouble as you thought. But you're gonna have to face the truth first, before you can accept it." Despite our hurtful exchange of only moments ago, she gives me what appears to be a smile of encouragement. "One time I saw a thing on TV about transvestites. Believe it or not, most of them are married and straight. Family men."

I kick off my sandals. "You expect me to accept that Stan has some uncontrollable urge to dress up like a woman? That's ridiculous! He's the most masculine man I've ever known. He'd rather die than—"

"Look at the facts," Dottie interrupts. "You find a bra in his pocket. Then you find e-mails from Lou Lou. Remember what that first one said? Something about dressing up for him and meeting him in public so Stan could see how easy it can be. I thought he meant how easy it can be not to get *caught* with another woman. But now I think what he meant was how easy it can be to *pass* as one."

I wish she'd be quiet. She makes sense. I don't want her to make sense. Curling up on the sofa, I clutch a throw pillow over my head, but it only muffles her voice rather than blocking it out.

"Then we see Lou Lou," she continues. "Lou Lou's boobs are the right size for the bra. We find out Lou Lou's a cross-dresser. Maybe he gave Stan one of his bras to try out since Stanny's probably not comfortable shopping in the lingerie department yet. Mystery solved."

Pressing the pillow tighter against my head, I recall

Lou Lou's second e-mail. *You were great.* Could he have been referring to Stan going out in public for the first time dressed like a woman? Was Lou Lou telling Stan he pulled it off?

No. I know my husband. Something like that would go against everything he is. Not only is Stan not in *touch* with his feminine side, I'm doubtful he *has* one.

When I pull away the pillow and sit up, Dottie is watching me. "You told me he shot out of his chair like a rocket and turned off the computer when you came up behind him. What was he doing on the computer in the middle of the night, anyway?"

"Dottie, please. I don't want to discuss this anymore."

"Just listen. There are all kinds of fetish sites online. Support groups. Stanny could've been looking for people to talk to incognito. People who'd understand what he's going through."

"He's not going through *anything!* Not like that."

"Let's go look on the computer. There's a way to see what sites have been visited over the past weeks. If we don't find anything, I'll drop it. I promise."

I shake my head. "No."

"No?"

"I'm not going to nose through his stuff anymore. I'm finished stalking him."

"You're throwing in the towel?"

"I'm going to tell him what we found out and give him one more chance to explain himself."

Dottie shrugs. "Okay. When?"

Shoving my feet back into my sandals, I answer, "Right now."

So far, my undercover work has dredged up more questions than answers. It's time for Stan to spill his guts and put an end to all the speculation. To tell the truth.

Whether it's A, B or C.

Stan is on the phone when I turn the corner into the cubicle that serves as his office. His face goes pale when he catches sight of me. I guess his neck's still stiff; he does his usual shoulder roll, complete with the wince and a left-to-right stretch of his neck. Too much time behind his desk? Or is the pain brought on by stress? A guilty conscience?

Continuing his conversation, he motions me to one of two chairs across from him.

Paperwork and two empty coffee cups clutter his desktop. On the other side of the flimsy walls, phones ring and voices mingle.

After Stan ends his call, he walks around the desk and leans against it, facing me. "How are you?"

"Okay." I look up into his eyes. "Terrible. Can we talk?"

He nods toward the door. "Let's go somewhere more private."

When I stand, he takes my elbow and leads me down the hallway to an empty room with a conference table in the center. Leaning against it, he crosses his arms. "I've been meaning to call you. Things have been crazy around here."

I step closer, place my purse on the table beside him. "I want to talk to you about something and I want you to be straight with me. I think I deserve that much."

He twitches and blinks, then nods. "Okay."

"And you deserve for me to do the same, so I'll just tell you right out that I followed that woman today."

"What woman?"

"The one I saw you talking to outside of Wong's."

"You—" A red flush creeps up from beneath his collar, and his eyes narrow. "How did you know where to find her to follow her?"

"That's not important." Maybe it's unfair for me to expect honesty from him without telling him I've tapped into his e-mail. But I know if I admitted that fact, it would end this conversation. He'd usher me out the station door without another word. "What *is* important, is that I talked to her."

"You talked about me?"

"No, nothing like that. We were at a nail salon having pedicures. I sat beside her. We made small talk, that's all." Or Dottie made small talk. But I don't want to mention my sister's name to him, considering his opinion of her. "Is there anything you'd like to tell me about that woman, Stan?"

"Didn't I already say that I would explain everything just as soon as I can?"

I glare at him.

"I told you before…" He blinks. "It's not your business, Dinah. Drop it, okay? That woman—"

"—Is not a woman."

All the color drains from his face, then rises again, twice as dark as before.

"The person I saw you with at Wong's is a man. A man dressed in drag." My voice quivers. "Does the bra I found in your pocket belong to *him* or to *you?*"

Stan turns his head, stares at the wall for almost a full minute. Then he faces me again, looks into my eyes and says, "What do you think? That I'm…" He looks away again, as if he can't bring himself to finish the sentence.

"Are you?" I whisper.

Before I can take another breath, Stan turns, grabs both my arms and pulls me to him. Crushing his mouth against mine, he forces my lips apart. At first,

I'm too startled to fight him. His kiss is so hard, our faces so close, that I can't breathe. When my senses return, I struggle, but it's a weak attempt, and he knows it. He knows my body, knows all the signs that I'm responding, that I want more, that I want *him*. When I start kissing him back, he loosens his grip on my arms, and I lift them to his shoulders and encircle his neck, my heart tapping out a wild cadence. A sound of longing that matches all I'm feeling rumbles up from deep in his chest. I break our connection, drag my lips from his and he scatters kisses on my tear-dampened cheeks, across my nose, my eyes.

"Does that answer your question?" he murmurs.

"It does, but—"

"You're the only one I want, Dinah. I love you."

No words have ever sounded sweeter, or filled me with so much relief.

He hooks my hair behind one of my ears and says, "That person you saw me with has information about a case we're working on. He's an informant. That's all I can tell you right now."

"At Wong's…she…*he* hugged you."

Stan looks sick. He blurts a laugh. "He's demonstrative. What can I say? If I'd known it was coming I would've run in the opposite direction."

I eye him warily. "But the bra…"

"That's all I can tell you right now," he repeats more firmly. "When the time is right, I'll explain everything, I promise. For now, you'll—"

"Just have to trust you." I smile and touch his cheek. "That's not easy for me. No one has ever given me any reason to trust them."

"Except me." He scowls. "Have I ever given you any reason *not* to?"

"Not until this happened. Can't you even—" When he squints, I say, "Okay, I'll back off."

"Promise me."

"He was only giving you information?"

"What did you *think* he was giving me?" Stan looks horrified and embarrassed all at once.

I wince and laugh. "I'm sorry. I didn't really believe it. I just—"

"Dottie put the idea in your head, didn't she?"

"Let's not start in on that again." I grin. "Besides, she was more inclined to believe you were *wearing* the bra."

Stan's face pales. Frowning, he coughs, scoots to one side and steps away from me. "How long is she staying?"

"Until after the baby is born." I wait a few seconds, then ask, "When are you coming home?"

"You two have things to work through. Considering the chemistry between your sister and me, it'll be easier if I'm not living under the same roof while you do it."

"You're not coming back?"

He lowers his gaze.

Stunned, I say, "But it's your home."

"Let's give it some time," he says quietly. "Pete's okay with me staying at his place for a while. Besides, I think you and I could still use some space, like we talked about."

"I don't need space," I whisper, panic and confusion churning inside me.

"Let's give it some time," he repeats. "I don't see how we can talk about things while she's there. I'll call you every day, I promise. We'll go out. Spend some time together, just the two of us."

"Why?" I catch his gaze, hold it. "I don't understand. Are we okay, or not? And don't you dare say I have to trust you."

"We're okay." He checks his watch. "I have to go. But I want that promise first. You'll back off, right?"

I scowl. "I'll back off."

"You'll quit prying into what isn't your business?"

"I thought you were seeing another woman, which would absolutely *make* it my business."

"*Dinah.*"

"Okay, okay. I promise."

"Good." He smiles. "Now come here and give me another kiss."

I'm torn as I step into his arms. He's using Dottie as a poor excuse to stay away. But why? He hasn't spent enough time with my sister to have so much animosity toward her; it doesn't make sense. I know in my gut that he has some other reason for not coming home.

"I'll call you later tonight," he says.

I blink up at him. "I love you."

"I love you, too."

When I arrive home, I find Dottie in the backyard at the patio table, a cigarette between her fingers. Hoot barks nonstop at a squirrel in the tree. Saxon hides in his doghouse, only the tip of his nose poking out.

She holds up the cigarette. "It's not lit, okay?" Sighing, she looks at it with longing.

I sit in the chair facing her.

"How'd it go with Stanny?"

"We were wrong. About everything."

With a skeptical frown, she leans back and says, "Let's hear it."

"Lou Lou is an informant on a case Stan's working."

Her brows lift. "And the bra?"

"There's an explanation for that."

When I don't elaborate, she says, "Okay. What is it?"

"He didn't say, but he insinuated that it's evidence."

"He *insinuated*." She makes a scoffing sound. "You let him get to you, didn't you?"

Drawing my lower lip between my teeth, I glance away.

"Let me guess how it went. '*I looooove you, Dinah*.'" She makes kissing noises. "'*There's no one else, baby. Only you*.'"

Heat creeps up the back of my neck.

"And you fell for it."

"I believe him."

"If the bra is evidence, then why wouldn't he just say so?"

"Because he can't. I suppose it's confidential."

"You *suppose*?"

"I trust him, Dottie. So give it a rest, okay?"

Staring at me, she lifts the cigarette in front of her face, rolls it between her thumb and forefinger, sniffs it. "Let me ask you this. In the five years you've been married to the guy, have you ever before found evidence for one of his cases in his pocket? Or lying around the house, even?"

Why does she have to ask the very thing that's been nudging the back of my mind ever since I left the station? The thing I've being trying to ignore?

"Aren't detectives usually more careful than that with their evidence? Good detectives, anyway?"

"I trust him," I say emphatically, but I can't help wondering who I'm trying to convince more—her or myself.

"Because?"

"He's my husband."

Dottie shakes her head and laughs.

"Why do you care so much about this, anyway? What does it matter to you?" Was I right in the car earlier? Is she jealous of my relationship with Stan? Does she want it to fail and prove that my husband is no better than the losers she chooses? Or is it something else? Something more? Something deeper than that?

"I don't give a shit what he's doing," she finally says. "Figuring it out just gives me something to do. Your little middle-class suburban cliché of a life is boring me out of my gourd." She lifts her brows. "No offense."

I stare at her for a long time. "If you're so bored, why don't you rent some more movies? You used to spend hours—"

"I'm tired of movies," she snaps, interrupting me. "I'm not a stupid kid anymore, okay? I quit looking for Mama in movies a long time ago." She appears startled by her own admission.

And that's when I realize we share more than a name and a past. We share the same heartache, identical wounds that, even after decades, are still tender to the touch. "So what do you suggest?" I ask quietly.

Dottie shakes off her stunned look, and one corner of her mouth curves up. "Let's go get our free drink at the Pink Slipper tonight."

I scowl at her. "No."

"Why not?"

"You're pregnant. You can't drink."

"I'll order a tonic and lime."

"I'm not going to The Pink Slipper." Not that the idea doesn't intrigue me. I want to trust Stan, to stay out of his business. But if everything he's doing with Lou Lou is on the up-and-up, why won't he come back home? Why did he even move out in the first place?

Dottie stands. "Fine. I'll go without you. First I need a shower and something to eat, though."

"You're not going anywhere. Did you take a nap while I was gone?"

"Listen." She plants a fist on one hip. "Just because we've made an agreement about the baby doesn't mean you can ground me like I'm a teenager."

When she starts for the back door, I stand and follow her. "Your baby is my responsibility, so I'm making it my business to see that you take care of yourself."

She opens the door. "Last I heard, tonic water won't harm a fetus."

"Please, Dottie," I say as the door slams shut behind me.

She pauses in the center of the kitchen and turns to me. "What are you so afraid will happen if I go there?"

My body tenses. "I don't know."

"What are you afraid I'll find out?"

"I don't know."

"I think you do."

Seconds tick away as we stare at each other. Finally, cursing under her breath, she breaks the cigarette in half, walks to the trash can and tosses it inside. "So, what are you in the mood for?" she asks in a resigned tone. "Hepburn and Tracy? Or Alfred Hitchcock?"

CHAPTER 11

On Saturday morning, Stan calls to say one of the
secretaries at the police station has two extra tickets
to a play at the local theater. The eight o'clock show.
Would I like to go with him? Stan hates plays but he
knows I adore them. During the five years of our
marriage, I have only managed to drag him to a
couple, so I'm flattered that he's willing to suffer
through one for my sake. Considering the invitation
a peace offering, I happily tell him I'll go.

I suggest we have dinner beforehand, and he claims
he can't make it that early.

The evening passes in awkward silence. As we sit
side by side in the darkened theater, instead of
watching the play, I watch Stan. By the end of the first
act, understanding dawns; he didn't want to go to
dinner because it would require that we make conversation. Here, we aren't free to talk, saving him
from a discussion about his plans to move home. The
baby. Us.

Despite his assurances when he kissed me at the police station, the image of his and Lou Lou's shared hug keeps pushing its way into my mind. I study him, searching for some sign of…I'm not sure. Deception? Guilt? A hidden fetish? I try to be discreet but, more than once, he catches me looking and his expression transforms from boredom to discomfort.

After a tense and quiet drive home, a choir of crickets serenades us as Stan kisses me outside our front door. Confused by his choices, hurt by his silence, I hold back a part of myself, refusing to melt into him like I did during our last kiss.

I hear Dottie's raised voice behind the closed door of her bedroom when I enter the house.

"It's none of your damn business where I am, Dave."

Dave. The piano-playing lounge lizard. Anxiety smothers me like a blanket on a hot summer day. I tiptoe down the hallway until I reach her room.

"It's your *right?* You gave up your rights when you tried to force me into a corner." A pause, then, "I don't give a rat's ass if that was before you knew. The only rules I live by are my own. If you don't know that, you don't know me." She groans. "Do I need to spell it out? *N. O.* You don't have a say, got it? This is my decision to make." Another pause. "You're damn right you'll stand by whatever I decide."

A sharp thud sounds as something hits the wall to the right of the door. I jump then raise my fist and knock. "Dottie? Are you okay?"

After a few seconds of silence, she answers, "I'm just dandy."

"You don't sound dandy."

The door opens. Dottie sniffs. Her eyes are puffy and red. "How was the play?"

"Long." Watching her, I walk into the room and sit at the edge of her bed. "You want to talk about that phone call?"

She scoops her cell phone off the floor. "There's nothing to talk about."

"That was him, wasn't it? The baby's father?"

"Don't call him that."

"Dottie…" I'd rather not talk about him, either, but I don't see an alternative. "Does he want this baby?"

"No, he doesn't want it. He's just using it as a way to get to me."

"To get to you how?"

"It doesn't matter. He's not a threat."

I stand and walk up behind her, place my hands on her shoulders. "If Dave Reno refuses to sign those papers, I can't adopt the baby. If that's a possibility, I want to know now."

"He'll sign," Dottie says, still avoiding my gaze.

"I hope you're right."

But the one-sided conversation I just overheard created something else for me to worry about. Even if he does sign, what if, later, he changes *his* mind and decides he wants the child? Hires some lawyer to find a loophole in the paperwork, something overlooked that reinforces his claim?

Later that night, I toss and turn in bed, my mind crowded with images from the nightly news. Crying, confused children taken from their adoptive parents after years have gone by, to live with birth parents that, to them, are strangers. In my fitful dreams, those children turn into Dottie and me during our first days with Aunt Maeve. Lost and wounded and bewildered. Watching the road for signs of Daddy, listening for the rumble of his car engine. Waiting. Always waiting. Crying ourselves to sleep at night in the room with the red curtain on the window, clinging to one another. Dottie's six-year-old face peers across at me from her pillow. *Don't you give up on me, too,* her innocent eyes seem to say. *Don't leave me. I need you.*

A shift, and then it's not her face, but another child's. Her baby's. Mine. But the eyes are identical to Dottie's, and the message they send is the same.

Don't you give up on me, too. Don't leave me. I need you.

* * *

Monday morning, I stand beside an examining table while Dr. Meryl Evans slides an ultrasound wand over Dottie's gel-coated bare belly. My pulse skitters as I watch the tiny screen in the darkened room.

"There," Dr. Evans says. "See it pulsing? That's the heart."

My breath catches. I laugh and press a hand to my own chest, feel the thump of my own beating heart.

"Here's the head. See it?"

"Does everything look okay?" I ask, my voice small and wary.

Dr. Evans glances at me. "The baby appears to be healthy and normal." Returning her focus to the screen, she smiles. "Would you like to know the sex?"

When I turn to Dottie, her head is flat against the pillow and, instead of watching the screen, she stares at the ceiling, chewing her gum, her expression blank. She hasn't uttered a sound throughout the entire procedure. Not a comment, not a laugh, nothing.

"Dottie?"

She looks at me.

"Do you want to know what it is?"

"That's up to you." Her voice is as detached as her expression.

Her demeanor confirms that she's made the right

decision about not raising the baby. Some women aren't cut out to be mothers, and Dottie apparently is one of them. I won't question her motives. Maybe that's out of respect for her, or simply selfishness on my part; I don't know. I don't care to analyze my silence too closely.

Nodding at Dr. Evans, I say, "I want to know."

"See here?" she says.

I squint at the place on the screen she indicates.

"It's a boy."

All the breath rushes out of me. All the love I possess rolls like a wave toward the life inside my sister. "A little boy."

With a laugh, Dr. Evans says, "He's sucking his thumb."

I don't know what draws my gaze to Dottie. For the past several seconds, I haven't thought of her, only the baby. And myself. But, now I look at her, and my world turns upside down.

She gazes at the screen now instead of the ceiling, her emotions naked on her face. Love and awe. Longing.

For the second time in as many days, I face the fact that we're not so different; I know now why she holds this baby at arm's length. Dottie fears she is a reflection of our parents, that she inherited their short-comings, just as she inherited Mama's eye color. I know this, because I've had that same fear about myself.

Dottie wants her son, but she's afraid she'll fail him. That's the secret she hides behind her mask of indifference. She has disconnected from this event as a means of survival, to protect her own heart.

It would be so much easier for me to continue believing she's callous, cold and selfish. That she has no feelings at all for the life inside of her. That she's unfit to be a mother. Then I could embrace this baby as my own and let my sister drift out of my life again, happy to watch her go. But I can't pretend not to see the proof that she loves her son; it shines too bright in her eyes to ignore.

I look at the screen again, torn between my own desire to be a mother, and the needs of a sister I'm just beginning to understand.

We're quiet on the drive home. I pull into the garage and we both go inside. The dogs rush in from the backyard when I open the door. Dottie excuses herself and heads for her bedroom, saying she wants to lie down for a while. Hoot Junior follows her, and I'm surprised when, with a sheepish glance back at me, Saxon does, too. He's had little attention from me over the past week, since I've been so consumed by the adoption and my problems with Stan. I can't really blame him for taking refuge with Dottie.

After changing into cargo pants and a T-shirt, I head out front to the mailbox barefooted. My next-door neighbor, Alice Eichner, a stay-at-home mom with a new baby, is at the curb checking her mailbox, too. "Hi, Alice."

She smiles and starts over, a stack of letters in one hand, a glass of iced tea in the other. "Haven't seen you in a while. You having a good summer break?"

"So far so good," I lie. "How's the baby?"

"Fun and demanding." What I guess to be dried breast milk stains the front of her white blouse. I glance up quickly when she catches me looking at it. "She's messy, too," Alice says. "I've given up on trying to look good."

I smile at her. "You look beautiful. You have that new-mother glow."

She laughs. "It's called exhaustion." Glancing at Dottie's Impala, she asks, "You have company? I saw the U-Haul."

"My sister."

"Oh, she must be the woman I saw pull up on that Harley the other day."

I doubt I'd be any more stunned if Alice had thrown her iced tea in my face. Forcing a smile, I ask, "When was that?"

"I'm not sure. Thursday, maybe."

The day we drove home from Aunt Maeve's then went shopping for maternity clothes. The day Stan moved out his things.

"You and your sister don't look a thing alike," Alice continues. "Where'd she get all that silky blonde hair?"

Wigs R Us, I think. *And he isn't my sister.*

My mind spins with questions. If Lou Lou is nothing more than an informant in Stan's case, why would he come to our house? And how convenient that it was on an afternoon when I was away. The very same day Stan moved out.

"Dottie's hair changes color from month to month," I say, struggling to keep my voice steady. "She didn't mention seeing you."

"I don't think she did. I was on the side of the house watering the flower beds. She went in and came right back out a minute later with Stan." Alice leans in closer, smiling sympathetically. "He seemed ticked off at her. I can relate. Scott hates it when my family comes to visit. They can't stand to be in the same room."

I change the subject, we chitchat and then I say goodbye and go inside.

Numb, I sit at the kitchen table and look out the

window, trying to think of one innocent reason an informant would come to a cop's house. Why would Lou Lou even know where Stan lives? It doesn't make sense.

Unless Stan lied to me, and Lou Lou is more than an informant. Which puts me right back where I was before Stan kissed me at the station.

In a state of confusion.

CHAPTER 12

Dottie

Hey, Peep. So, you're a boy. That's not news to me. The first time you punched my intestines like a boxer and kicked my ribs like a soccer ball, I guessed you weren't a prissy little girl.

Not that all girls are prissy like Dinah; I wasn't. Even now, I could teach you to throw a baseball. Hit one, too. I held the home run record at Coopersville elementary school for six years straight. I even skunked the guys. And I was never afraid of bugs or snakes or anything else, like Dinah is. It wouldn't bother me if you brought home a frog. But, hey, you'll probably have a great time making her squeal. Put a big fat lizard under her pillow for me while you're at it, okay?

Speaking of lizards, Dave called last night, saying he loves me and he wants me to come back to him. Wants *us* to come back. He said he was bluffing when he told me we were through if I didn't marry him. He thought I couldn't live without him, so I'd agree to tie the knot. That shows how little Dave Reno understands Dottie Dewberry. If a man, or anyone else, wants to hit the road, I say good riddance. I've been dumped all my life, and I always manage to get by. I'll get by without him, too. So much for his big plan. I know a thing or two about bluffing.

Which brings me to something I want you to know. I was bluffing by pretending that giving you up will be easy. I'm not dumping you, Peep. I'm giving you a better life. Better than you could have with me, Dave or no Dave. He and I are a couple of screwups without anything to show for the lives we've lived except the world's biggest collection of regrets. What do I know about raising a kid? I'm selfish and restless. I'd do everything wrong and you'd end up hating me. Better to cut the tie now instead of later after it's too late and I've messed up your life. I know how parents can do that, believe me. This is the best thing for both of us, you'll see.

God, I could sure use a smoke. You're making my life miserable, Peep. And keeping me on a guilt trip. I know it's bad for you, but I'm having a hell of a time quitting. Don't ever start; it's a bitch. Some nights I dream about tobacco and I wake up smelling it. Craving it. Sometimes I catch myself reaching for a cigarette and thinking one won't hurt. Usually, I resist, but not always. See? Some mother, I'd be. Putting my needs before yours. But, hey, I never asked for a kid. And I only gave in one day this week. Not bad for a chain-smoker, huh?

Speaking of bad habits, what's up with the thumb sucking? That'll ruin the shape of your mouth, did you know that? You'll have to have braces on your teeth if you don't stop. But you looked kind of cute with your little hand all curled into a fist and pressed close to your mouth like that.

I never imagined that you'd already be so perfect, a mini person, complete with all the parts, even the one that, if you grow up to be like most guys, will get you into a lot of trouble down the road.

I wonder if you'll have Dave's dark eyes. They're drop-dead beautiful eyes, Peep. The color of coffee and always smiling. I know if you'd been a girl, you would've wanted his long, dark lashes, for sure. No Maybelline needed with lashes like those. I hope you have his dimples. You'd be better off with my nose, though. Dave's has a bump the size of Pike's Peak in the center of the bridge.

I keep putting together all kinds of combinations, mixing my features up with Dave's in a dozen different ways to imagine how you might look. Let me tell you, I've come up with some pretty funny faces. Plenty of handsome ones, too, though, so don't you worry about it. However you end up looking, you'll be you, and that'll be fine. Dinah will love you and always do right by you.

I just wish... Well, never mind what I wish. When you get right down to it, what Dinah can give you is all you'll ever need.

CHAPTER 13

Dinah

On Tuesday, my attorney, Robert Rutson, sits across his desk from Dottie and me in his sunny downtown office.

"How long will it take for the adoption to go through?" Dottie asks, sitting stiffly, her hands clasped in her lap.

"I'll go ahead and have the papers drawn up relinquishing yours and Mr. Reno's rights," he explains. "Then after the baby is born and they're signed, the judge might want a short hearing just to wrap things up." He lifts a shoulder. "Shouldn't take much time. Only five or ten minutes."

The leather squeaks as Dottie shifts in her chair, her brows pulled together. "Me and Dave will have to be there?"

"You can both attend if you'd like, but only Dinah's presence is required."

With a nod, she turns to the wall of windows

beside her, lifts a hand to her mouth and nibbles her thumbnail.

Robert catches my gaze. I know what he thinks. Dottie's rigid posture and troubled eyes reveal her uncertainty.

"Do you mind if my sister and I have a word in the hallway, Robert?"

"Of course not." He slides back his chair and lifts his coffee mug. "You can stay in here, though. I need a refill."

When he leaves, closing the door behind him, silence hangs heavy in the room. It's time to stop pretending to Dottie, and to myself, that I don't see the truth. "You're sending out signals that you're not sure this is what you want to do."

"I'm sure."

It's tempting to let it go at that. To assure myself I gave her the chance to change her mind. To grab this opportunity at motherhood and not look back. But I know if we get any further into the proceedings and it all falls apart, I might fall apart, too. And then there's the matter of Stan and what my next-door neighbor Alice revealed. Am I crazy and selfish to bring a baby into my mess of a marriage?

"Why do you really want to go through with this adoption, Dottie?"

"I told you. There's no room in my life for a kid."

"You could make room. Parents do it all the time."

"I'm not parent material."

"Why do you think that?"

"I know myself. *You* know me." She tilts her head. "Have you changed your mind?"

"No, but I do have some worries."

"Okay. What?"

"I'm afraid after you see the baby, you'll…" Emotion swells my throat. "I already love him, Dottie. If you back out now, it'll hurt me, but it won't hurt half as much as it will if you wait until after I've held him in my arms. And I'd *never* recover if you waited years and then came back to take him away."

"I'd never do that to you," she says quietly.

I wish I believed that; I want to believe it. But after all we've been through together, I've learned to expect the worst from my sister. Could she really have changed so much?

"I'm not the same person I was," she says as if reading my thoughts.

"What about Dave Reno? I overheard the end of your conversation the other night. He said something to you about his rights."

"He won't fight this. He'll do whatever I say."

"Then what were the two of you talking about?"

"He—" Her voice is unsteady. "He wants to get married."

"But you said he was a one-night stand."

"I lied."

"Why?"

"I don't know. So you wouldn't worry about him coming around, I guess."

"Do you love him?"

She hesitates a fraction of a second too long to be believable before shaking her head no.

I give her a skeptical frown. "If you love each other—"

"I'm not the type to settle down. Not with a man *or* a kid." She smiles a little, but I see desperation behind it. "I'd get antsy, you know that. I'd want to move on."

Like our mother. She doesn't say the words, but I hear them, anyway.

A reassurance that she's better than Mama almost slips past my lips, but would she believe it? Do I? They share so many parallels, Dottie and our mother. For too many years, I've placed them in the same category. But I've never imagined Patsy Dewberry struggling over her decision to leave her children as Dottie so obviously struggles with hers. Did Mama? Or was leaving us easy for her, the selfish act I've always thought it to be? An impulse. The truth is, Dottie *isn't* deserting her baby, like Mama deserted us.

"Maybe it would be better for everybody concerned if someone else adopted your son, Dottie. Someone you don't know and never will. Dave, either. Then there'd be no going back and no one would get hurt." Except, I know it's already too late. I'm already hurting, and so is she.

"Please," she whispers, panic flashing in her eyes. "I want *you* to be his mother. I couldn't give him to a stranger."

A mix of affection, pity and dread sifts through me. What am I walking into? Whatever it is, I'm in too deep to climb out now.

I reach for Dottie's hand. "Let's go find Robert and tell him to draw up those papers."

We eat lunch at a buffet downtown, then head home. An old yellow Camaro sits out front of the house behind Dottie's red Impala. She curses and groans when she sees it.

"You know that car?"

Her face pales. "It's Dave's." Flipping the visor down, she checks her lipstick in the mirror.

"I was afraid of this," I mutter.

"Drop me off in front."

I pull alongside the Camaro and stop. The driver's door opens and a small, thin, swarthy man with dark burred hair steps out. He has a tattoo on his left bicep, below the sleeve of his black T-shirt; I can't make out the design. His jaw is set, his eyes squinting.

Wary, I almost stop Dottie when she begins to roll down her window. Then Dave Reno recognizes her in the passenger seat, and he breaks into a grin, exposing a mouthful of Tom Cruise teeth and the deepest dimples I have ever seen.

With the window down, Dottie proceeds to call the man everything but his name. "I thought I told you to stay the hell away from me."

"I tried, baby." Sunlight glints off his gold neck chain. Kneeling, he props his forearms on the windowsill and I see that the tattoo is a heart with *Mary me Dottie* written inside. The name Mary is a different shade of blue ink, more faded than the rest of the sentence. I bite back a smile. *Clever guy*.

Dave Reno looks across at me, and something in his eyes softens me on contact. I find myself thinking that Mary, whoever she is, was a fool to let him slip away.

"You must be Dinah," he says.

I start to respond, but before I can, Dottie snarls, "How'd you know that?"

The crackle of her anger doesn't appear to concern him. "Maeve told me."

"Aunt Maeve? How'd you find her?"

"You told me you had an aunt in Coopersville, baby. Remember? I took a chance and called information for Dewberry." He laughs. "She's a pistol, that one."

"Yeah, and I'm about to jam her trigger." Dottie throws open her door and almost knocks the man over. The door slams shut. "Give us a sec, okay," she calls to me over her shoulder.

"I'll be in the house," I say.

As I put the car into Drive again, Dottie's friend moves her aside and leans into the window, offering me his hand. "I'm Dave Reno, by the way."

"I figured as much. Nice to meet you." We shake, then he scoots out and faces Dottie's fury.

I don't envy him.

Ten minutes later, Dottie walks into the kitchen.

"Where's Dave?"

"He went to find a motel room. He's picking me up at seven tonight and we're going to eat. I have some things to say to him, but I want to cool down first."

"I don't see that happening by seven," I mumble.

"He thinks I won't commit murder in a public place." Her tone implies he's wrong to make that assumption.

But something about her irritation seems forced and insincere, at odds with her expression. My lip twitches. "He's not what I expected."

"What did you expect?"

"The way you talked about him? A slimeball."

"What makes you think he's not?"

"Eyes don't usually lie, Dottie."

She melts like butter in a microwave, her green eyes dewy beneath her fringe of bangs. Then, just as quickly, her gruffness returns and she says, "Oh, yeah? Well, I've known a lot of slimy men with great eyes."

Amused, in spite of my uncertainty over what Dave's arrival might mean, I leave Dottie to entertain herself while I work on my article the rest of the afternoon. At six, I stop to heat up a bowl of leftover vegetable soup. The doorbell rings at six-fifteen.

Dave stands on the porch holding a bouquet of wilted pink carnations. His dimples wink at me.

"You're early. Dottie's in the shower."

He shrugs. "I couldn't wait."

I invite him into the kitchen and give him a glass of ice water. Laying the bouquet on the counter, he joins me at the table while I eat my soup and crackers.

"Here's the deal," he says after a few silent moments filled only with the sound of my spoon clinking the edge of the bowl. "I usually just tell it like it is."

"I like that."

"Good, 'cause the thing is, I love your sister."

"Does she know that?"

"If she doesn't, she's as deaf as she is hardheaded." The space between his brows creases. He fingers the gold chain at his throat. "What happened to make her so afraid of getting close to anyone?"

"She's been hurt." As much as me; I'm beginning to understand that.

"Damn it, the woman loves me. I know she does. But she backstrokes if I mention the *m* word."

"Then don't mention it. Why not just live together?"

"She won't have that, either. You know how tired I am of either wakin' up at my place alone or at her place without my toothbrush?"

I grin. "Your teeth don't look like they're suffering."

"Maybe not, but *I* am."

Why hasn't my sister grabbed this man? Is there something I'm missing? Is he a snake charmer? A con artist, and I'm falling for his game? As fine-tuned as Aunt Maeve's radar is, surely she would've picked up on that, even on the phone. Aunt Maeve wouldn't have sent Dave here if she thought he was bad news.

I take a breath and ask, "Do you want this baby?"

He rakes fingers across his burred head. "Well, I didn't exactly cry tears of joy when Dottie told me the news. I'm forty-eight years old. I already have two grown daughters. A granddaughter, too, for chrissake. But it's ours, so, sure. I want it. I want the whole package. The baby and her, too. But it's her call to make. If she wants me to sign papers giving up my rights, I'll sign papers. And I won't bother you again. Or the kid."

"Why would you do that?"

"Can't see myself raising it alone at this stage of my life. It wouldn't be good for either one of us."

"Did she tell you it's a boy?"

"No." Blinking, he looks out the window and releases a noisy breath of air. "Imagine that. A son. Never had one of those."

Dave Reno is no con man. I can tell by the wistful sound of his voice, the sadness and regret in his eyes. My heart twists for him. And for myself.

"Why are you here, Dave?"

"To try to—" He looks past me, then stands.

I turn to see Dottie in the doorway, wearing a khaki pantsuit we purchased in the maternity department of Dillard's.

Dave whistles. "You look like a million bucks, baby."

"I look about as sexy as a lumpy pillow." Dave extends the bouquet of carnations toward her. Surprised pleasure flashes in her eyes, then disappears just as quickly. She dismisses the flowers without a second look. "I won't be long," she says to me. "Dave's gonna buy me a steak, and I'm gonna set a few things straight with him. Then I'll be home."

They leave me frustrated and confused. What if he convinces her to go back to him? To keep their son? I try to push aside what I want, and ask myself, instead, what's best for everyone concerned. If the answer is Dottie and Dave together, raising him, then I should be happy with that.

So why do I feel as wilted as Dave's carnations?

I awake with a start to find Dottie standing at the side of my bed. The lamp is on, the book I was reading facedown on the comforter beside me. I sit up and rub my eyes, look for Saxon, but he's not around. He is probably in Dottie's room with Hoot. Even my dog has deserted me, it seems. "What time is it?"

"Almost midnight."

"Took you longer than you thought to set things straight, I guess." I brace myself for the news.

"I told Dave to go home." She sits on the bed beside me.

"He told me he loves you."

"Well, I don't love him."

I don't believe her for a minute.

"We're never going to be a happy little family in the suburbs."

"Do you really think he's going to tuck his tail and go back to Vegas because you say so? He doesn't impress me as the sort of man who gives up on what he wants so easily."

"Well, this time, he better."

I yawn. "So where have you been so late?"

"I thought we'd have one last hurrah, so we went to The Pink Slipper."

"You *what?*"

"Lou Lou says hi."

That name is a kick in the ribs. "Why would you go there?"

"Why not? It's a public place. I was curious." She slips off her shoes, avoiding my gaze. "You talk to Stan today?"

"Yes. This afternoon. Why?"

"No reason. How come you two didn't get together tonight? With me gone, you could've had some privacy. You know, to talk."

"Last time we spoke, he said he was playing baseball tonight with his team."

Her brows lift. "He did, did he?"

"What's with the interrogation, Dottie?"

"Why isn't he coming home now that you two made up? Have you asked yourself that?"

Constantly, but I won't admit it to her. I haven't told Dottie what my neighbor, Alice, said. I wanted to think it through without any pressure from her. As much as I resist the possibility, I've been mentally going back over my years with Stan to see if I missed any clues that he might be gay. So far, I haven't stumbled upon so much as a hint that my husband and I share the same sexual preference.

"Think about it. Now that you've agreed to quit dogging him and the two of you have kissed and made up, why would Stanny stay away? Because of me?"

"He said he wanted to give us some time together alone to work out our differences."

"That's a cop-out." She snorts. "No pun intended."

"Let's talk about this tomorrow, Dottie. I'm tired."

Ignoring me, she says, "Just because I'm staying with you, he moves out? Would you pack up and leave if one of his relatives came for a visit?"

"He doesn't have any relatives. Well, only a cousin. But they aren't close."

"I'm making a point."

In an effort to veer her on to another subject, I say, "I think his name is Lawrence."

"Who?"

"The cousin. He and Stan grew up together but he left town right out of high school after his parents and Stan's died in a car wreck together."

Dottie doesn't take the bait. "I think you're being duped," she says.

I stare hard at her. "What if Stan would've spotted you at The Pink Slipper?"

"How could he spot me there if he's playing base-ball?" She looks smug. "See? You don't believe him, either."

"He might've had to drop by after the game to talk to Lou Lou again or something."

Dottie shrugs. "So we run into each other. Happens all the time." She laughs. "I can't remember when I've had so much fun people-watching. And Lou Lou's a scream! You should see him dance."

No, thank you. Please.

"He gave me more drink tickets, by the way. And a free pass to get me and a friend in next time without paying a cover."

"There's going to be a next time?"

"I hope so." She nudges my leg with her hand. "Let's go one night this week. It'll cheer you up."

"What makes you think I'm not cheerful?"

"What did you do tonight?"

"Nothing." Except look at my wedding photos and

cry. I kept staring at Stan's smile and wondering if he was wishing he wore my white lace dress instead of his suit.

"See? You're in a rut. Let's go have a few laughs tomorrow night."

I'm tempted. But what if Stan is there with Lou Lou? He'll think I followed him again. And that would be the end of us. No questions. No explanations. "I can't go there, Dottie. The only reason we even know about The Pink Slipper is because we were stalking Stan. I promised him I'd stop nosing into his business."

"Since when is going out for a drink nosing into his business? Like I said, it's a public place, and it's a free country, too. Besides, Lou Lou invited you."

She stands and starts from the room.

"Did you give Robert's name and number to Dave so he can call with any questions he has about the adoption?"

Dottie pauses beneath the doorway. "Dave doesn't have any questions. He said the decision's up to me."

Regret tinges her voice, but I choose to pretend that I only imagine it.

CHAPTER 14

I'm pouring my first cup of coffee the next morning when the doorbell rings. I glance at the clock on the oven—8:00 a.m. Apparently Dave Reno's an early riser.

He's who I expect to find on my front porch. Instead, I find Aunt Maeve.

"'Mornin', lemon drop." Carrying a small suitcase and a slouchy fringed suede bag, she floats in on a wave of sandalwood and cinnamon, her bracelets jingling.

Since my aunt never shows up uninvited, I ask, "What brings you here?"

"Dottie called last night and said you're down in the dumps."

"What time did she call you? She didn't get home until midnight."

"That's when the phone rang." Aunt Maeve lifts the case. "I brought some things to pull your spirits up by the bootstraps." She winks. "We're gonna have ourselves a little makeover day. The face paint's in here. The wigs are out in the Beetle. Some girlie fun oughta cheer you right up."

"I'm not depressed." But my voice sounds drab and flat, even to me. "What did you do? Leave Coopersville at the crack of dawn to get here?"

"I left at seven."

"Where's Babe?"

"At home. Lynette next door's keeping an eye on her. I can stay for as long as you need me." Aunt Maeve settles on a kitchen bar stool, her short legs dangling, then asks me about Dave Reno.

Before I can answer her, Dottie walks in and says, "I sent him packing."

"Good God-a-mighty, girl, have you got a screw loose? That man's a keeper."

"How do you know?" Dottie asks. "You've never laid eyes on him."

"No, but I talked to him for a good hour and a half on the phone. I got a seventh sense about voices." Aunt Maeve hops down from the stool and heads for my pantry, her leather sandals slapping her feet. "Where's your tea, Dinah? I'll read Dottie's leaves so she'll know—"

"There's not gonna be any tea leaf readin' on my account," Dottie says, headed for the refrigerator. "When it comes to Dave, I know all I need to know."

"Don't be mule-headed," my aunt barks. With her hand paused on the pantry door, her kohl-smudged eyes suddenly flutter closed. Drama trickles through her harsh voice, softening it to a deep, flowing timbre as she says, "Three swirls of the tea, Dot, quiet your mind...let your soul guide you toward the right path." Opening her eyes again, she focuses on Dottie. "You'll see. It's the same path Dave walks, and it leads to a diamond ring and a two-car garage."

"That's what I'm afraid of," Dottie says dryly.

Pulling open the pantry door, Aunt Maeve mutters, "Foolish damn girl."

Dottie rolls her eyes at me, then opens the fridge and takes out a soft drink can.

Without a word, I walk over, remove it from her hand and replace it with a carton of yogurt, receiving a scowl in return. "Why'd you come over so early?" I ask my aunt. "Don't you have appointments today?"

"I canceled them," she says then snaps, "This tea won't do." Shoving my jar of sugar-free instant back onto the shelf, she closes the pantry door.

"You canceled before you left this morning? I pity the poor people who got a phone call before the sun came up."

Aunt Maeve clears her throat. "I wanted time to talk to you girls." She looks from Dottie to me and back again. "Your daddy called yesterday. He wants to see y'all."

I pour a cup of coffee for Aunt Maeve, add creamer to it and stir, taking my time.

"You mean on July fourth?" Dottie's voice is wary. I feel her gaze on me.

"Sooner," Aunt Maeve says. "As soon as you'll agree to it, he'll come out."

Dottie sighs. "Where's he living?"

"Who cares where he lives?" I put the cup down on the counter in front of Aunt Maeve so hard, coffee sloshes over the sides. "So now we're supposed to drop everything and have a meeting with the man because he decides he's got time for us?"

Dottie's eyes flash. "He came before. To your graduation. You treated him so mean you drove him away." She sounds like the hurt little girl I remember from long ago. The one who used to cry herself to sleep beside me.

"I treated *him* mean?"

She sniffs the yogurt and frowns. "Well, you didn't welcome him with open arms, that's for damn sure."

"Why would I? Why would you? Anyway, that was over twenty years ago, Dottie. He hasn't even tried to contact us or see us since. Doesn't that tell you anything?"

"I want to see him. I told you, I have questions."

"Why is it so important that they get answered all of a sudden? Because of the baby?"

She doesn't reply, only stares at me.

"What you don't deal with in this life," Aunt Maeve says, breaking the silence, "has to be dealt with in the next one, or the one after that."

Dottie nods. "That's right, and I don't want to come back to this same old heartache again. I don't want Daddy to have any part in any of my lives after this one. I want good men around me. The kind who'll treat me right."

I'm glad to hear she knows she deserves better. Still, I shake my head. "That's the craziest reason I've ever heard."

As I sop up the spilled coffee with a paper towel, Aunt Maeve reaches across the counter and stills my hand. "I understand how you feel. But would it hurt to give him just a minute? Your daddy might want to make amends."

"Is that what he told you?"

"He didn't say why he wanted to come. Just that he needed to see his girls."

"His girls," I scoff. "He's more than three decades too late for that."

She squeezes my fingers and says quietly, "I'd like

to see my big brother again. One more time. I can't say why, but when I heard his voice, I had a feeling this might be my last chance."

"Dottie and I don't have to be there for you to see him."

"I don't think he'll make the trip if you're not."

"Quit being so selfish," Dottie snaps at me as she moves around to my side of the counter. She gestures at Aunt Maeve. "Think of her for once instead of yourself."

Ashamed and confused, I toss the paper towel in the trash, then cross my arms.

"He hurt me, too," Dottie says, her voice gentle now. "I feel the same way you do about him. But if he finally wants to talk, I've got to listen. And I need you with me."

She needs me. Like always. My stomach knots as I say, "I'll think about it."

I manage to hold Aunt Maeve and her cosmetic brushes at bay until late afternoon by taking her to look at paint samples for the nursery. When we can't agree on a color, we swing back by the house to pick Dottie up and go to lunch.

Now, after setting up beauty shop around the kitchen table, Aunt Maeve lines our lips and eyes, applies false eyelashes, uses a pencil to color in a beauty mark at the side of my mouth and to darken Dottie's brows.

Dottie chooses a long, curly brown wig. I choose a short, spiky red one.

Their laughter and joking brightens my dark mood and, for a time, I forget my questions about Stan, my worries over the baby, my irritation at Daddy's request.

I shriek when Aunt Maeve lifts a mirror in front of my face. "Who *is* that?" I look as funky as Dottie looks exotic. "Would you recognize me if you passed by me on the street?"

Dottie snorts. "I wouldn't." She stares into her own handheld mirror. "I wouldn't recognize me, either."

"How did you do this, Aunt Maeve?"

With a chuckle, she looks askance at me, her eyes too bright and, when she speaks, the emotion in her voice takes me off guard. "I've had years of practice, honey."

Of course, she has. I should know. I was there. I allow the memories to come out of the dark, and recall other days like this one. Playing dress-up with Dottie and Aunt Maeve. I always loved it; we all did. It was one of the few things the three of us enjoyed doing together. I remember one day in particular, gathered around the kitchen table in the trailer house on a snowy afternoon. Aunt Maeve made hot cocoa,

the closet door, Aunt Maeve hoots and whistles and Dottie tells me how sexy I look. I soak up their affection, thirsty for it. I think I have been for a very long time. Which makes me sad, since I know it has been waiting, mine for the taking.

Maybe I will go out with my sister, let this recaptured feeling of connection with her continue. Maybe I'll turn a few heads, feel desirable for a change instead of dragging my butt around, moping, waiting for Stan's phone calls, wishing he cared enough to come home and tell me what's going on in his life.

Less than an hour later, Dottie has on a billowy chiffon number and spike heels that show off her shapely calves.

Aunt Maeve shoos us out the door, tells us to have a little fun, yawns and says she's too "worn-out" to go with us, but she'll stay and share Dottie's bed tonight in the guest room, if that's all right.

We're halfway to The Pink Slipper before I crash down from my high and start to get antsy. What was I thinking, anyway? The only heads we might turn will be those of gay men who think we're men in drag, too. "I'm turning around," I say.

"No way." Dottie frowns at me. "I'm not watching

any more movies. We're going to have some fun for a change."

"I have a weird feeling about this."

"Relax. Chances are, Stan won't be there. If he is, he won't recognize us, anyway. Not unless we talk to him."

I glance at my reflection in the rearview mirror. "You don't think so?"

Her eyes narrow as she glances across at me. "You're really afraid he might be there, aren't you?"

I take a deep breath, then tell her what my neighbor said about Lou Lou coming to the house on the day we came back from Coopersville.

"That does it," she says, slamming the heel of her hand against the dash. "I'm going in even if you don't. This has gone on too long, and he's being mean, keeping you guessing. He should just confess so you can get on with your life."

Her exasperation and concern for me sound genuine, and I admit to myself that I don't know how I would've gotten through the past week and a half without her.

When I readjust the mirror, Dottie says, "Your hands are shaking." She nods at the giant neon-pink slipper over the door of the building up ahead. "You ever been to a place like this?"

"No, never."

"Get ready. Lou Lou isn't the only man in this town who wears a skirt." As I pull into the parking lot, Dottie winces and laughs. "Too bad most of them don't have his legs."

A large square bar, surrounded by tables on three sides and a dance floor on the fourth, dominates the center of the club. A song about shaking your "groove thang" plays, and several couples do just that. Some of the men in the club are dressed like women, some aren't. A few couples appear to be straight; men with women. We find an empty table and sit. I thought Dottie and I would stand out like two yellow crayons in a box of reds, but no one gives us a second look.

The walls sparkle with pink sequins. Heavy pink draperies cover the windows. Pink feather boas edge the backs of every chair.

Dottie is in her element. All smiles, she snaps her fingers and sways to the beat of the song. She pauses long enough to wave a waiter in a curly platinum blonde wig and a long strapless red evening gown over to our table, then orders a ginger ale. "What about you?"

I consider my usual martini. But Stan makes them best, and thinking about that stirs too many emotions in me, so I order a ginger ale, too, then watch the waiter walk away. "If not for the black back hair, he could pass for a woman," I say to Dottie.

"Lou Lou said it's an employment requirement that the waitstaff dress in drag." Sitting straighter, she waves at someone behind me. "Oh, look, there he is." Dottie waves Lou Lou over, but when she catches sight of my expression, she lowers her hand and says, "Oh, shit. I'm sorry, I wasn't thinking. You gonna hold up?"

"I'll be fine." I'm more confused than anything else about the person headed toward us. Confused and wary and hurt.

Lou Lou looks as perplexed as I am. He pauses beside the table and purses his fuchsia lips. "Welcome to The Pink Slipper, sweeties. I'm sorry, I've forgotten your names."

"It's me. Dottie. From the nail salon? And I came here last night with my friend Dave. Short weasel of a guy? Big teeth?" She gives a startled laugh and presses a hand to her head. "Oh, I forgot the wig! No wonder you don't recognize me."

Lou Lou leans in and looks closer. "Oh, yes! Dottie! Where *is* that gorgeous man of yours?" He tsk-tsks and adds scoldingly, "Weasel, my patootie."

"He couldn't make it, so I brought my sister,

instead. Remember her? She was with me at the nail salon."

"Well, of course, I do!" He slides into the chair beside mine.

I resist the urge to scoot away from him. It's all I can do not to ask him point-blank what he and Stan are up to behind my back.

Eyeing me, Lou Lou says, "You had on a hat at the salon. You should never cover up that fabulous hairdo."

"It's a wig," I say, trying not to snarl.

"I'd love to borrow it sometime." He wiggles his arched brows. "The cleavage is a nice touch, too."

"Sorry," I say dryly. "I can't loan you that."

Laughing, he offers me his hand. "I don't think we introduced ourselves the other day. I'm Lou Lou Andrews."

"Dinah," I say, and we shake. His hand is soft and smooth but, when I glance down, I see that it's a masculine hand. Only the red manicured nails are feminine.

I see questions in his eyes when I glance up again, and I suspect he wonders if I'm *that* Dinah. Stan's wife. So I add, "Dinah Dewberry," as a precaution and watch relief ease the tension from his face.

"You girls should come back some Sunday night for the floor show. It's quite a production. We draw a big crowd."

"You have a good crowd tonight, too," Dottie says.

Lou Lou smiles. "Business has been wonderful."

Dottie scans the room. "Can I be blunt?"

"Please do."

"I'm sorry, but I just don't get it." She gestures at a couple on the dance floor. "The one in the miniskirt is a man, too, right?"

"Yes. That's Pat. And Greg. They're good friends of mine," Lou Lou says. "Why?"

Dottie frowns. "If a man is attracted to other men, why would he want his partner to dress like a woman?"

Lou Lou looks at his watch. "Sweetie, how much time do you have?"

Laughing, Dottie nods toward the bar. "That bartender wasn't working last night, was he? The one with the black shaggy layered cut? He looks familiar."

"Oh…Stella. She's new, poor baby. She moved here a couple of weeks ago from L.A."

"I used to live in L.A. Maybe I knew him—I mean *her*." Wincing, Dottie gives an apologetic smile. "Which is it, anyway? I mean, what should we call all of you?"

With a coy tilt of his head, Lou Lou says, "Just call us *fabulous*."

I make an effort to laugh along with them.

"*Her*, sweetie," Lou Lou says, composing himself. "Address us as females. At least when we're at the club."

Dottie nods. "Maybe I'll go say hello to Stella and see if I can place *her*."

"I'd rather you didn't. Do you mind?" Lou Lou's tone is confidential. "She might be uncomfortable if you recognize her. Stella's rather new to all this. She's fresh from a divorce. The wife didn't take it well when she found Stella wearing her panty hose."

"She didn't know he's a transvestite?"

"Stella's not a transvestite, sweetie. Transvestites just play dress-up, they're not true queens."

"There's a difference?" Looking baffled, Dottie asks, "But he's gay, right?"

Lou Lou laughs. "Is a pig pork?"

Dottie groans. "I'm *so confused!* So *all* of the men here are gay drag queens? None are transvestites?"

"All of the *staff* are gay." He motions toward the dance floor. "As for our patrons, I couldn't say. I don't know all of them."

While Lou Lou talks, I watch the bartender mix drinks and I sympathize with his ex-wife. What a shock to find out something like that about your husband. *Not Stan*, I think. He doesn't belong here. He'd be repelled by this scene. Not that he has any animosity toward gay people; his motto has always been *to each his own*. But this isn't him. There *must* be another explanation for his behavior. For Lou Lou being at the house. I only wish I could think of one that made sense.

A waitress with a frosted beehive, rhinestone-encrusted eyeglasses and a frilly white apron pauses alongside our table. "Lou Lou, I'm dead on my feet," he says in a deep, gravelly voice. "Can I take a fifteen-minute break?"

"Sure thing, sweetie." Lou Lou stands and takes the tray from the waitress. "I'll fill in for you." He motions to us. "Christy, meet Dottie and Dinah."

Dottie asks Christy to join us as Lou Lou threads his way through the crowd.

"Girl, there's nothing I'd like better." Settling in Lou Lou's empty chair, Christy pulls a pack of cigarettes from his apron pocket, then says, "Is it okay if I smoke?"

"Only if you blow it in my face," Dottie says in a deadpan voice.

Christy cackles and, while they chat about the horrors of trying to kick the habit, I nibble my cuticles and watch Stella. The poor guy doesn't have the female bit down yet. He's not as smooth and polished as the others. His lipstick is smeared and he moves with about as much grace as an orangutan, bumping into the other two bartenders, stumbling on his high heels when he walks around the bar to pick up a glass he dropped, scratching his crotch when he thinks no one is looking.

What a loss for womankind, I think, despite the itch. A big, strapping, broad-shouldered guy like him, attracted to men.

"No, go on," Christy says to Dottie, then blows a smoke ring into the air. "Ask me anything. It don't bother me."

Dottie props an elbow on the table, breathes deeply. "When did you first get the urge to dress up?"

"I must'a been seven or eight. It was after I caught my old man wearing my mother's only good dress when she was working the late shift one night."

"I bet that was hard on you," Dottie says.

"Girl, you can't even imagine. That's one reason I never wanted kids. It ain't fair to 'em."

I try to concentrate on their conversation, but my mind drifts back to Stella. I glance again at the bartender. He sets a beer mug down on the counter then winces and rolls his left shoulder, stretches his neck side-to-side.

Goose bumps scatter up my arms. I scoot to the edge of my chair and study Stella's face. Wide, ruby-red mouth, long narrow nose, tiny cleft center chin. My heart drops. "Oh, no." I press my palm over my mouth. Perspiration pops out on my brow. "No."

"Dinah, what's wrong? Are you sick?"

"It's Stan," I whisper.

"What?"

I glance at her then over to the bar again. "Stan."
I almost choke on the name.

Sliding out of my chair, I run toward the rest rooms.

CHAPTER 15

A man wearing a pencil-thin black skirt and a pair of black leather slingback pumps I'd swear I took to Goodwill last year waits outside the men's room, but the women's room is empty. I glance back at Dottie before I go inside, and find her heading toward me. Behind her, the waitress who joined us at the table is squinting at Stella.

Dottie reaches my side, and we go in the rest room together. She locks the door. "What's wrong?"

I hug myself to stop shaking. "Stella is Stan."

"Stella? You mean that ugly, clumsy bartender? The one I thought looked familiar?"

I start to cry.

"Wait here." She reaches for the doorknob.

"No!" I catch her wrist. "What if he recognizes you?"

"In this getup?" She points at her wig. "Your husband's only seen me two or three times in his whole life. Maybe if he was looking for me he'd recognize me, but if that's him out there, I'm the last thing on his mind."

Chewing my lower lip, I let go of her. "Don't get too close."

"I won't. Just close enough." She unlocks the door.

I reach to stop her again.

"*What?*"

"You haven't seen Stan much, either. He has a mole on top of his right thumb. A freckle, really."

"You want me to look for a freckle on his thumb but not to get too close?"

"It's a dark freckle." I unzip my purse, dig around in it and pull out a pair of sunglasses. "Here. Wear these so he can't see your eyes."

"Right. They'll hide my eyes, but not his freckle. Gotcha."

Ignoring her sarcasm, I say, "Disguise your voice and order a drink. A strong one."

"I'm pregnant, remember?"

"For *me*."

Dottie takes the glasses and steps out.

I lock the door again and start pacing. What does this mean? That Stan *is* Lou Lou's lover? Or is he just a transvestite?

Oh, God.

Numb with shock, I bury my face in my hands. Up until these past few days, no one could've convinced me that I'd be relieved to learn that my husband is *just a transvestite*.

I remember Lou Lou's claim that all of the Pink Slipper's employees are gay, and a sob shudders through me. *Please, Stan. Please tell me Lou Lou's wrong. Give me a believable explanation for the wig, lipstick and heels.*

Maybe that won't even be necessary. Maybe Dottie will come back and say that I was mistaken; Stan isn't Stella. They just share the same neck quirk, the same chin cleft, the same nose and mouth. It's possible.

I cry harder.

It seems like an eternity before a knock sounds at the door, and Dottie says, "Dinah, it's me."

I let her in and she hands me a glass. Without bothering to ask what it is, I take a long drink. The liquid scorches my throat and burns a pathway down to my stomach. Lowering the glass, I say, "Well?"

She's quiet for several seconds then says, "Look at the bright side. Gain some weight or have Stan lose some and you two can share clothes and double your wardrobe."

My lip quivers. "That's not funny."

"I know." She hugs me. "I'm sorry. What do you want to do?"

I squeeze my eyes shut, squeeze her. "Let's go home," I whimper.

* * *

Aunt Maeve's snores echo down the hallway when we tiptoe into the house.

Dottie pauses beside the table. "You want to talk about this?"

I pull off my wig and toss it onto the counter. "No. I can't."

"You sure?"

I nod.

"Then I guess I'll go to bed. Not that I'll get any shut-eye with all that racket Aunt Maeve's making." Starting from the room, she glances back and says, "I'm all ears when you're ready. I won't even crack any jokes." She lifts two fingers. "Scout's honor."

"You were never a Scout."

"Or honorable." Her smile is sad and sympathetic. "But I mean it. If you need me—"

"Don't go," I say, sniffing. "Stay in my room tonight. I don't want to be alone."

She appears surprised and pleased. "Sure, if that's what you want. I'll go wash up and put on my gown first. It won't take a minute."

In my bedroom, I open my lingerie drawer, skim my fingers across a pink satin gown. Stan's favorite. When I wore it, I always thought he liked what was *underneath* it most of all. Was I wrong? Did he envy me getting to wear it? Did he put it on when I wasn't home?

Shoving the gown aside, I try to block out all the bizarre, troubling images that keep flashing through my mind. I grab a long cotton jersey, shut the drawer and head for the shower, asking myself if our marriage was nothing but a cover for him. Did he ever really love me? Does he love me now? How can Stan make love to me as he does and still be...whatever he is?

Hot water beats down on my face. I wish it could wash away every trace of this night along with my makeup. After a minute, my heartbeat slows as the water soothes me, and I begin to think clearly for the first time all night.

Trust me. Stan's constant plea. But how can I? What possible reason could he have for tending bar at a gay nightclub dressed in drag, other than the obvious one? Did he lie when he said Lou Lou gave him information about a case? Or does his *case* have something to do with him being at The Pink Slipper? Try as I might, I can't reason that out. Stan quit working undercover long before we ever met.

I dry off, put on the jersey then find Dottie curled up on my bed.

"You look exhausted," I say.

"I'm just a little tired."

"You didn't get your nap today. That's not good." I turn off the light and climb under the covers beside her. After a few moments I say, "Stan and I met at a fourth of July picnic. A friend of mine named Jolie Conrad invited me. Her husband, Pete, is a cop, too, and they were already married. Before Pete got shot and resigned, he and Stan were partners." I sigh. "All these tough guys were playing volleyball with their shirts off and their muscles glistening with sweat."

"Oooh...like that beefcake scene in *Top Gun?*"

"Pretty close." I smile. "There wasn't an unattractive one in the bunch, but even so, Stan stood out. God he was gorgeous. Every inch male."

"He still is," Dottie says. "Your husband's a head turner."

"He turned my head back then, that's for sure. He turned it again tonight, too, but not for the same reasons." I swallow a rising sob. "Once, Stan and I were on a date, and I saw him risk his own life to save some people he'd never met from a house fire. We were driving by and saw the flames. The fire department wasn't there yet and his training kicked in. You should've seen him, Dottie. I fell in love with him that night."

After a long silence, Dottie says, "I've been thinking... Could Stan be working undercover at The Pink Slipper?"

"That crossed my mind, too. But he hasn't done that sort of thing since he was promoted from SWAT to Detective. Even if he hadn't been promoted, he swore he'd never take another undercover assignment."

"Why?"

"His fiancée, at the time, couldn't stand the danger and the hours. Sometimes he was gone days at a time. That's what broke them up. Shortly after that, he was knifed during a drug sting and he almost died. That was the final straw."

After a minute of silence, Dottie says, "I keep thinking about his e-mails to Lou Lou and the ones Lou Lou wrote back to him. Remember how dull they were?"

"I know. I still feel like there's more to all of this than what it seems."

"What do you want to do now?"

"Try to get some sleep so I can worry about this tomorrow." I roll onto my side and, for at least five minutes, maybe longer, listen to the ticking clock on the nightstand beside me. "How did you meet Dave?" I finally ask.

For a long time, she doesn't say anything, then, "Like I said, he played piano at one of the bars in the same hotel where I worked. After my first day on the job, I stopped by for a drink with another casino waitress. I heard his music before I saw him. He was playing 'My Funny Valentine.' Remember Mama singing that to us?"

I do, but I'm surprised she does. Dottie was so young when our mother left.

"Dave played it so smooth it brought tears to my eyes."

"I thought you said he was a lousy piano player?"

"I only said that because he made me so damn mad before I left Vegas." She's quiet a few moments before adding, "He's not a lousy lovemaker, either."

"What did he do to make you so mad?"

"He said if I didn't marry him, we were through."

"Knowing you were pregnant?"

"He didn't know yet. I didn't know."

"Why are you so dead set against marriage, Dottie?" When she doesn't answer, I say, "It's because of how Mama and Daddy were with each other, isn't it?" When she still doesn't answer me, I take a deep breath. "You're not Mama, Dottie."

"No, but I'm like her." Her voice is a thin wisp of regret.

"Just because you've heard that all your life doesn't make it true. Sometimes Aunt Maeve doesn't think before she speaks. Anyway, I'm sure she doesn't mean you have Mama's bad qualities, only her good ones. You know, her looks and her love of the spotlight."

"That wasn't such a good quality. It took her away from us. Besides, Aunt Maeve also says I talk like her and walk like her and—"

"All her good traits," I repeat.

"You can't deny I got her impulsiveness, too."

"But *you* haven't let that hurt anyone but yourself."

"I hurt you," she whispers. "And I'm sorry for that."

My chest tightens, and I'm slapped again by the memory of that night in Austin long ago. But the sting isn't as sharp as it once was, and I realize I'm over it. That I've forgiven my sister. "It was one mistake, and you've apologized, which is more than Mama ever did. What happened then doesn't compare to what she did to us. We were babies. We depended on her. It was her duty and her privilege to take care of us and she turned away from it like it didn't mean anything. She failed us."

"That's why—" Dottie's voice cracks. "I'd fail, too. At being a mother, I mean."

Going still inside, I touch her damp head, hurting for her. I acted ashamed of her when we were growing up; often, I *was* ashamed. All those times I rescued her, it was as much for my own sake as hers. I didn't want anyone to know that my sister had screwed up again.

In my mind, her failures, her bad behavior, spilled over onto me. No wonder she never learned to take care of herself, to do the right thing; she had me to fall back on. No wonder she was terrified of me marrying and leaving her behind. No wonder she doesn't trust herself to succeed at the most important thing in her life.

All these years, I've thought Dottie to be selfish for all she expected of me. The truth is, I've been selfish, too.

"You're not Mama," I whisper, then try to erase the pretty picture I've painted in my mind. A baby boy with Dottie's face, asleep in my arms, calling me his mother. "You can do this, Dottie. If you want it bad enough you can be a good mother. I know you can."

The next morning Aunt Maeve tells Dottie that Dave called the night before while we were out. Three times. Envy tweaks when she doesn't mention a call from Stan.

At ten, a driver delivers a basket of sweet pea blossoms for Dottie. Refusing to look at it, she tells me to read the card. It says,

To Dottie, my sweet pea. I'll take you however I can get you, baby. Married or not. Night and day, every day, or weekends only. Just please don't give me the shaft. I need you. Love, Dave.

"That's so romantic," I say to her, biting my lip to avoid smiling over Dave's amusing way with words.

"Sweet pea," Aunt Maeve says in her leaf-reading voice. "Lathyrus adoratus…fragrant pulse. Blissful pleasure. Seeds sewn between the feasts of Saints David and Chad and of Saint Benedict produce larger blossoms." She hoots a laugh, and with her loud Texas drawl returning declares, "I'm bettin' on an August wedding if he can hold out that long."

Mumbling words that would make a rock star blush, Dottie reaches for the card I hold, tears it in half, presses the pieces into Aunt Maeve's hand, then plops on the couch to watch *Judge Judy*.

At eleven-thirty, the hamburger joint around the corner delivers three Frito pies, three cold Corona beers and a container of limes. Scrawled across the top napkin inside the sack are the words,

Dottie, thought this would remind you of our first date. No Frito pie can satisfy my hunger, baby. Only you. You and your family enjoy the meal. Love, Dave.

"Idiot," Dottie grumbles. "He doesn't even know pregnant women can't drink beer." She dumps half of her pie into Hoot's food bowl and the other in stirred in cinnamon, then turned us into beauty queens. We dug through her jewelry box, a small velvet-lined glass case from the dime store filled with tangled multicolored trinkets. She threaded strings of fake pearls through our hair, pinned sparkling broaches on to the shawls she draped over our shoulders. We slipped into her high-heeled shoes that, at the time, were still too large for our little-girl feet.

Why did I ever give that up? Say no to my sister and aunt when they wanted to play, wanted to draw close and love me? Why did I let myself grow so serious so soon?

Dottie primps her curls with her fingertips, her eyes dancing. "Let's get dressed up and go kick up our heels. I'm sick and tired of sitting around this house."

My emotions are strung tight, but I don't want her to know. "You went out last night," I say struggling to keep from bursting into tears.

"I'm used to being out *every* night."

"No wonder you don't have any money."

Though I protest and grumble, I let Dottie lead me to her bedroom, let her hold in front of me a skintight knit dress cut low in the front to show cleavage and high in the hem to show thigh, let her talk me into trying it on, since it's too snug for her pregnant body.

As I stare at my image in the full-length mirror on

Saxon's, then returns to the television to watch *Passions*.

Shrugging at each another, Aunt Maeve and I clink our bottles together then pick up our plastic forks and dig in.

After lunch, Dottie lies down for a nap while Aunt Maeve and I leave to shop for baby clothes. Though Dottie hasn't given me any indication that she's changed her mind about our deal, I set aside my previous plans to buy paint for the nursery. Clothes can travel if Dottie decides to take her son with her when she leaves here. A painted room can't.

Aunt Maeve turns up her nose at some of the dressy little outfits I show her. "Too fussy. This, a few T-shirts, gowns and socks for his feet is all he'll need," she says, holding up the tiniest overalls I've ever seen. "A kid needs room to breathe. Not some highfalutin straitjacket."

On the drive home, I say, "You think Dottie will change her mind and keep the baby?"

"Can't say." She shrugs. "I haven't read her leaves yet."

"You don't need leaves to know what she really wants. Even I can see it."

"That's true enough. But I also don't need 'em to know the thought of giving her heart to a man and raising a child scares that poor girl to death. Sometimes fear is stronger than desire."

"Why do you think she's so afraid?"

"She thinks she's failed at everything else, and she's convinced she'd fail at family life, too," Aunt Maeve says, confirming my suspicions.

"Like our parents did."

She shoots me a sad glance and nods.

I clear my throat and say what's on my mind. "I wish you'd stop telling Dottie she's like our mother. She's heard that all her life. Not only from you, but from me and everyone else in Coopersville who knew Mama."

Aunt Maeve's cheek twitches and her brows draw together. "Oh, honey…I never meant it in a bad way. I adore you girls. I'd never mean to hurt you."

"I know that—so does Dottie. But I can't help wondering if she heard herself compared to Mama so much that she felt she was destined to make the same mistakes."

Aunt Maeve stares straight ahead out the window. "I did the best I knew how," she finally says, her voice quiet and full of self-doubt. "Some folks accused me of letting you girls run wild. They said you needed more structure. Maybe you think so, too. Maybe Dottie does. And maybe everyone's right. But I'm not sorry. If I'd tied the two of you down with rules and done everything for you instead of letting you fend for yourselves some, you wouldn't be the women you are today. And you're good women. Both of you. Oh, I know Dottie has her problems, and maybe the way I raised y'all played a part in that—"

"You aren't the cause of our problems, Aunt Maeve. We always knew you were there for us. I hate to think where we'd be now if you hadn't taken us in."

"I know growing up like you did wasn't easy, Dinah."

"Is growing up easy for anyone?" I laugh a little. "We didn't make things easy on you, either. You didn't ask to have two kids dropped off on your doorstep."

She blinks at me. "That may have been the worst day of your life. Dottie's, too. But it was the best day of mine."

Stunned by her declaration, I blink at her, tears in my eyes. "I love you, Aunt Maeve." So easy to say. So true. Why have I kept the words hidden away, tied up tight inside of me? "I hope you're aware just how much."

"I love you, too, lemon drop. As if you were my own child. You're about to find out for yourself how that feels. Once you lay eyes on that sweet little baby, you'll never be the same again. He'll be yours, just as much as if you'd made him yourself. You'll do the best you can with him and love him like crazy. That'll be enough."

I don't tell her I'm as certain as I've ever been of

anything that Dottie is the person who will lay eyes on the baby and never be the same. Dottie will do her best with him and love him like crazy. And it *will* be enough.

As I turn onto my street and see another florist's van parked in front of the house, I sense that my sister's life is about to take a wonderful turn. That possibility swells my heart with happiness for all she stands to gain.

And with sadness over what I stand to lose.

CHAPTER 16

Thanks to Dave's parade of deliveries throughout the day, I'm able to avoid discussing Stan and what I'm going to do to either save or end our marriage. Good thing, since I don't have a clue. At dinner, Dottie finally brings up the subject.

She stabs a carrot. "What do you plan to do about Stan?"

Aunt Maeve sets down her glass of lemonade and watches me.

"I want to go back," I tell Dottie.

Her fork pauses halfway to her mouth. "To The Pink Slipper?"

I nod. "I was too shocked last night to take it all in. I want to watch him and see how he is with the clientele. You know…is he comfortable with them? Does he fit in? Or is it all an act?"

Maybe it's the wrong thing to do. The sneaky thing. The thing I promised to stop. But why should he expect more from me than he's willing to give in return? He lied and said he'd be playing baseball last night. If working at The Pink Slipper has something to do with a case he's on, why didn't he just say he had to work late and leave it at that? He could've left out the part about the wig and the makeup and the fact that he can't walk worth a damn in high heels.

"Smart girl." Dottie rubs her palms together, looking eager and excited. "So we'll dress up again, right?"

I glance at Aunt Maeve. "Are you up for another lipstick and eye shadow session?"

She smiles. "Always."

"I'd invite you to go with us, but he'd know you in a minute, disguised or not. Besides, you've got too much hair to stuff under a wig."

"The dogs and I will be fit as fiddles right here."

Dottie has a tough time finding another outfit to disguise her pregnancy. Aunt Maeve's billowy black silk poncho solves that problem. By the time she's in her long, dark wavy wig, her eyes smudged with kohl and the shawl in place, Dottie looks like a sexy witch. I, on the other hand, look like a middle-aged punk rocker again with my spiky red hair.

At 10:00 p.m., we pull into The Pink Slipper's parking lot. As we head for the door, Dottie says, "I'm so glad you thought of this. I can't wait to take a deep breath of that smoky air."

Tonight, we choose a table that gives us a better view of the activity behind the bar. There's no sign of Lou Lou or Stan, and I immediately start to worry that our efforts will be unrewarded.

Soon, Christy, the waitress who joined us on her break last night, appears at our table. Tonight his glasses are pink and he wears a fifties poodle skirt with a white blouse tucked into it. "If you two keep showing up, you'll give this place a bad reputation for going straight," he teases in his low growl, his grin revealing a mouth full of crooked teeth.

"We haven't found anyplace as much fun," Dottie teases back. "Everyplace else is too stuffy."

"What's your poison tonight?" he asks.

Dottie orders a tonic water and lime. I order a martini. "Extra dirty," I tell him. "With four olives and a lemon twist. No vermouth."

He chuckles. "My kind of gal."

"Where's Lou Lou tonight?" Dottie asks him.

"In back doing paperwork. She'll be out later."

"What about that bartender from last night? Stella…I think that was her name." I glance toward the bar. A different bartender with blond braids tied in bows serves beer to a man wearing a fringed white leather skirt and red ankle boots with spurs.

"Stella should be here any minute." Christy eyes me over the tops of his glasses. "Why?"

I shrug. "She mixes a good drink."

He lifts the order pad. "I'll make sure she gets this then."

As Christy turns away from our table, Stan walks through a doorway that leads to a back room and hobbles toward the bar. He wears a shimmery gold pantsuit and platform shoes that would easily break an ankle if he fell off of them. The long, straight black wig he wears is pulled back from his face tonight.

I nudge Dottie.

She murmurs, "Hubba hubba," snickers, then mouths *sorry*.

Another waitress reaches Stan before Christy does, and hands him an order slip. Christy rips the sheet of paper from his order pad, hands it to Stan, too, and says something to him. Stan chuckles, glances over to our table at the same time Christy does, and waves.

My heart drops and Dottie gasps, but Stan turns and starts filling the first order without giving us a second glance.

With sighs of relief, Dottie and I both sink back against our chairs. "Christy must've told him we complimented his work or something," she says.

A curvy brunette wearing an evening gown approaches our table. "Welcome back. I'm Josephine," he says in a sultry voice. We make introductions. "I saw you two in here last night." He looks us up and down. "Let me guess. This is the straight table, right?"

"You could say that." Dottie laughs.

Josephine places a white-gloved hand on his hip. "Would you like to dance?"

"Maybe later," Dottie says. "We have drinks coming and I'm dying of thirst."

Raising one painted-on brow, he shifts to me. "How about you?"

I consider it. I've never danced with a man who is dressed as a woman. Depending on what happens with Stan, there's a chance I might have to get used to it. "Maybe later," I say. "I feel a little queasy." *Every time I look at Stella.*

"I'm sorry." Frowning sympathetically, Josephine presses a palm against my forehead. "No fever. That's good." He smiles. "You rest up and I'll check on you later."

As Josephine leaves, I return my attention to Stan. He sets drinks on a tray and the first waitress comes by and takes it away. Then Stan reads our drink order on the slip Christy gave him, and his head jerks up. He stares across at us.

"Oh, shit," Dottie breathes. "*Look* at him. What did you order?"

Lifting a hand, I nibble my cuticle and avert my gaze. I whisper, "I think it was my usual."

"Which is?"

"An extra dirty martini with four olives, a lemon twist and no vermouth."

"I filled a lot of drink orders in my day," Dottie says, "but never that one."

Stan continues to stare. When Christy approaches him, they talk for a minute, then Christy puts his tray down and steps behind the bar.

Stan's mascara-coated eyes narrow as he approaches Dottie and me.

This is it, I think. The moment of truth. I stand and face him. "What's going on, Stan?" I ask in a quivering voice when he stops in front of me. The close-up sight of him as a woman repulses me, but I try not to let my reaction show.

He glances from me to Dottie and back again, a blush creeping up his face and beneath the edge of the wig. "Follow me," he says quietly, then leads us to an empty table. We sit. Stan scans the room then says in a low voice, "I thought you agreed to stop following me?"

"I didn't follow you. Lou Lou gave us free drink

tickets the other day at the nail salon, and we decided to use them. I didn't expect to find you here. Especially not dressed like—" I turn away from him, no longer able to hide my revulsion. I feel as if I've stepped into a bizarre nightmare where everything is strange yet familiar at the same time. The person in front of me is a stranger, yet he's not. He's a painting of Stan left out in the rain, his image warped and water-smeared almost beyond recognition.

Stan glares at Dottie. "Why are you two in disguise if you weren't trying to hide?"

She smirks at him. "We could ask the same question of you, Stanny."

"Lower your voice," he hisses, then looks around as if making sure nobody's listening to us. "Don't use my name."

I lean toward him. "Aunt Maeve came yesterday. We played dress-up. That's how we got the idea to come here." I force myself to stare into his face. "Look at me."

Stan keeps his gaze lowered to my chin.

"Look at me," I repeat. When he finally does, I say, "If you don't tell me what you're up to, I'm going to assume the worst."

Another blush penetrates his thick layer of makeup. "You know me better than that."

"I thought I did. I'm starting to wonder. This—" I

sweep an arm down his front "—could explain all the secrecy. The jumpiness. All the late nights on the computer. What were you doing? Cruising transvestite and gay chat rooms?"

"*Be quiet.*" He looks over his shoulder, then back at me, frowning. "How do you know about those?"

"Dottie told me."

He slings his ponytail over his shoulder and huffs, "That figures."

Dottie snickers.

"What's so funny?" he barks at her.

"I'm sorry, Stella. But you make one butt-ugly woman." She presses her lips together then says in a barely controlled voice, "If you two will excuse me, I think I'll go shake a leg with Josephine."

Stan gives her a hard stare. "Don't mention me, understand. Not one word to anyone about this."

"Gotcha, Stella." Dottie weaves her way across the room.

Stan glances toward the bar where Christy makes drinks. "I'm here until 2:00 a.m. Barring any disasters, I'll come straight to the house after that. I'll explain this then."

I cross my arms. "I don't want to wait."

"Damn it, Dinah, I can't talk here. I'm already

going to have to make up a story about you to tell Christy. Go home and take Dottie with you. I'll see you after my shift."

I'm in my gown, pacing the bedroom floor when I hear Stan's truck pull through the alley behind our house. He walks into the room seconds later, and my heart dips to have him here again. In our house. Our bedroom. His wig is off, but he still wears the makeup and the feminine clothes.

"Sorry about this." His face flushes as he indicates the outfit. "I usually go straight to the station and in the back way after I leave the club. I shower and change there. But I didn't want to keep you waiting." He motions to the bathroom. "You mind?"

I cross my arms. "No. Go ahead. I'll wait."

Fifteen minutes later he comes out barefoot and shirtless, wearing a pair of old jeans he didn't take with him when he packed his things. His hair is damp, the makeup gone.

He sits on the bed. "You and your sister could've thrown a major kink in an investigation tonight, Dinah. I hear you came last night, too. And that Dottie was there the night before with some man."

I nod. "Dave. Her boyfriend." He continues to stare, as if waiting for more information, so I add, "Tonight's the only night we came to watch you, Stan. I swear. I was telling you the truth when I said that we only went the first time out of curiosity. We wanted to see a drag club, and we had free drink tickets. Then last night...when I recognized you..." I shake my head. *What is going on?*"

He sighs noisily. "I'm working undercover trying to catch some sick bastard who's threatening The Pink Slipper's staff."

"But you don't work undercover."

"I asked for this assignment. It's personal."

"I don't understand."

"Lou Lou is my cousin, Dinah."

"He's—?"

"Lawrence. Remember? I told you about him. He's all the family I have left."

I search my memory. "His parents were killed with yours in the car wreck."

Stan's expression is grim. "A month after our high school graduation. We were like brothers growing up."

"You said you two weren't close. There was nothing for him here after his parents' death so he left, right? And you lost touch after that."

Stan clears his throat. "That's only partially true. We did lose touch after he left. I saw to that. Lawrence and I *were* close growing up. Then, after our folks died, he told me he was gay, and I couldn't deal with it. I felt like he'd kicked me in the teeth when I needed him the most. Like our whole childhood together had been a lie. I said some things…" Stan looks away. "It wasn't a pretty scene, the night he left."

"Why didn't you tell me?"

"I don't know." He shrugs. "I guess I was ashamed."

"Of him?"

Stan nods. "Of myself, too. Maybe most of all."

"You knew about my history with Dottie. Did you think I'd judge you? I was ashamed of her, too. I shunned her."

"You had a right to. She walked all over you. She made a scene at your engagement party. Lawrence never did a thing to me."

"I'm not excusing what you did to him. Just saying that I'm as guilty as you. Maybe I pushed Dottie into treating me badly."

"I think that goes both ways, from what you've said."

We watch one another. "So Lawrence came home."

"About six months ago. He contacted me. I didn't exactly roll out the welcome mat." His face pales with shame. "Then, a month ago, I hear that a local drag queen name of Lou Lou Andrews was kidnapped. When they said he owned a nightclub called The

Pink Slipper, I knew it was Lawrence. The son of a bitch blindfolded him and took him to an abandoned warehouse on the outskirts of town. He brutalized Lawrence for two days."

"Oh God…" My stomach clenches.

"I don't know how he got away. Lawrence doesn't, either. The whole thing's a fog to him. He was in bad shape when he got to us." Stan's voice rumbles with anger and frustration. "We have a hunch the kidnapper is the same guy who killed a couple of drag queens in Oklahoma last year, and three others in Louisiana and Mississippi the year before that."

"A serial killer?"

He nods. "I'm going to catch the guy, Dinah. If it's the last thing I do. I promised Lawrence." For a moment, he lowers his gaze. "Will and I started frequenting online chat rooms. Getting familiar with some of the regulars. I struck up a friendship with a guy who meets the profile. He says he hangs out at The Pink Slipper. Calls himself Peter Pan."

"What does that mean?"

"Who can say for sure? He told me his father was gay and that he cross-dressed. Almost all of the victims so far were fathers. According to the profiler, in this guy's own mind, he might think he's avenging kids who are going through what he did."

"By murdering their dads?" A shudder ripples through me. "In other words, he's insane."

"He thinks he's justified. That he's a hero, even. He becomes more loose lipped the friendlier we get. He thinks I have a family. A wife who divorced me when I came out of the closet. Two kids. I talk to him about how the boys just can't accept what I'm doing, and he commiserates with me. He wants to meet me at The Pink Slipper to give me pointers to help win the kids over, like his father did him."

"He's laying the groundwork for you to be his next victim." When Stan doesn't respond, I ask, "What are you planning?"

"The meeting's all set."

"But, you've been working there. If he's been hanging out, won't he recognize you as Stella?"

"Will's going to meet him. I'll be there to watch over it from the bar. If Peter Pan's our man, he'll try to get Will to leave with him."

"When's this all supposed to take place?"

"Tomorrow night."

I sit on the bed beside him. "I'm afraid for you."

"That's the reason I don't like to talk to you about my work. You worry too much." Pushing a strand of hair behind my ear, he says, "My job can be dangerous. There's no getting around that."

I brush a kiss across Stan's lips.

"Lawrence is family," he says. "I may not get him, but I've missed him."

Thinking of Dottie, I whisper, "I know."

Stan leans me back against the pillows and props up on his elbow beside me. He strokes my cheek with his forefinger. "Do you understand now? I couldn't tell you all this. You have to quit following me around. Lives hang in the balance. Mine, Will's and everyone who works at The Slipper. If you and Dottie get caught up in it, yours, too."

"But why did you have to move out?"

"Until we catch this guy, I thought it'd be best. You were pretty damn insistent about getting involved. Then Dottie showed up. I figured she'd egg you on." His smile is sheepish. "Besides, I was embarrassed. I would've rather you thought I was seeing another woman than find out about me dressing in drag."

"That's silly."

"I wasn't sure I could look you in the eye again."

"You're looking now." I give him a coy grin. "See? I'm still hot for you, despite the fact that your cup size is bigger than mine."

He scowls at my teasing. "Do you know how damn

nerve-racking it was coming home to you after Lawrence started training me? I got so flustered I started making stupid mistakes. Like leaving that bra in my pocket. If I stayed here, I was afraid I'd slip up again. You're scary when you're jealous."

"Not many wives *wouldn't* be jealous of a cup size like that," I tease. "And you have beautiful eyelashes. What kind of mascara do you use?"

I blurt a laugh when he grabs my wrists, pulls them over my head and pushes them into the pillow.

"Tell me," I say, grinning up at him. "Did you get any propositions from the *girls?*"

"I'll show you a proposition," he growls, then kisses me hard. Lifting his mouth slightly, he murmurs, "What do you say?"

"Come back here," I whisper.

He releases my arms, and I wrap them around him. I don't let go.

CHAPTER 17

We sleep in the next morning. Later, while Stan showers, I wander into the living room where I find Dottie stretched out on the couch watching *Back Street* starring John Gavin and Susan Hayward, one of our mother's favorites. Dottie's feet are propped in Aunt Maeve's lap and Aunt Maeve is painting a tiny pink daisy on each of her toenails.

"'Mornin', lemon drop. You sleep okay?"

"I did."

"Where's that good-lookin' husband of yours?"

"He's in the shower."

Dottie looks up at me with puffy red eyes. "This movie always sets me off, but this is the worst time yet. I can't quit blubbering."

"Baby hormones," Aunt Maeve mutters, leaning back to admire her handiwork.

I glance to the center of the coffee table where a small cactus with a single pink bloom sits in a clay pot. "From Dave, I presume?"

Dottie nods, rolls her eyes and mutters, "A cactus. What's he trying to say? That I'm thorny?"

"A cactus stands for endurance." Aunt Maeve stays focused on Dottie's foot. "He's sayin' his heart will always burn with love for you."

"He's obviously crazy about you, Dottie," I say.

"No, he's just crazy." She avoids eye contact.

"He said he has grandkids."

"Two."

"So he's already raised a family?"

"Hardly. He barely sees his daughters. They live in Seattle. He and his first wife split when the girls were young and then Dave moved out to Vegas."

Is it a coincidence that Dottie hooked up with a man who left daughters behind? For the first time since Dave's smile charmed me, I'm concerned about his character. Why wouldn't he have stayed closer to his family? Didn't he want to be a part of their lives? Didn't he want them in his?

As if Aunt Maeve reads my thoughts, she says, "Could be he needed a fresh start in a new place. And, who knows, he might've thought there'd be less friction for his kids if he and the ex weren't living so close. Dave might have done what he felt was best for his girls."

"Or maybe he just screwed up," Dottie says with cold frankness.

Aunt Maeve glances up at her briefly. "Maybe so. Humans do that. But they can change. Try to right their past wrongs."

She isn't fooling me. We're not just talking about Dave anymore. We're talking about Daddy.

Dottie's eyes narrow. "His kind never changes. You shouldn't give him so much credit, Aunt Maeve. Dave left his family because that's what he does. He walks out when things don't go his way."

Our family tradition. He'd fit right in with the Dewberrys. Dottie can accuse Dave all day long, but she's guilty of the same thing. She walked out on him, didn't she? Just what we need in this family—another member with a penchant for running from problems.

Aunt Maeve blows on Dottie's toenails then asks, "Are we talking about the same Dave Reno who is buying out the florists in this town trying to win you back? Even though things aren't going his way?"

Dottie scowls. "I bet you wouldn't be so quick to defend him if you knew what I know about him."

"So, tell us," I say.

She studies me, and I can't help wondering if, by airing Dave's dirty laundry, she's attempting to prove that the baby is better off with me.

"For starters," Dottie says, holding my gaze, "Dave's done time."

"Who are you talking about?" Stan enters the room wearing old clothes, his hair damp from his shower.

Beaming, Aunt Maeve reaches for Stan's hand as he approaches and answers, "Dottie's boyfriend."

"Dave Reno," Dottie adds. "He lives in Vegas. Run a rap sheet on him, Stanny. Then tell Dinah what you find."

We eye each another. Nice smile and oodles of charm, or not, she's planted a seed of doubt in my mind about Dave.

"How are you, Stan?" Aunt Maeve asks.

"Good, Maeve." He bends and kisses her on the cheek. "How are you?"

"If I was any better, I'd make myself sick." She nods in the direction of the kitchen. "I made coffee. Help yourself."

Stan must remember how bitter Aunt Maeve's coffee is. "I'll grab a cup at the station," he says with a glance at his watch. "In fact, I'd better run."

Dottie lifts one foot toward him and wiggles her toes. "Sure you don't want to stay awhile, Stella? Aunt Maeve would be happy to paint a couple of daisies on your big toes." She flutters her lashes at him. "They'd really snaz up those platform sandals of yours."

Stan sends her a barbed look. "When you were

telling me about all your jobs, you forgot to add comedian to the list." He sets his jaw. "You two stay put tonight, you hear?"

I walk to his side, take his hand. "We aren't going anywhere."

"Make sure they don't," he says to Aunt Maeve.

I walk him to the back door. "Be careful. Call me when it's over."

"Just as soon as I can." He kisses me then says, "What's the deal with this Reno character? He's not bothering you, is he?"

"Don't worry about him. He may have a history, but he seems harmless enough to me."

"So did Ted Bundy."

"Actually, I sort of like Dave, but Dottie's pretty much told him to hit the road."

"For once I'm on your sister's side. I'll check up on him."

Something tells me that if we do go through with the adoption, Stan will run a rap sheet on every friend our son brings home.

"Quit pacing," Dottie says later that evening as she throws empty Chinese food cartons into the kitchen trash can. We ate on bar stools at the counter since wigs cover my table. Aunt Maeve works on one now, an ash-blond flip with bangs that she's currently covering with a fog of hair spray.

"You're on pins and needles," she says.

"I will be until he calls."

"That'll probably be hours from now." Dottie rinses her hands at the sink, then turns off the faucet and faces me. "It's barely dark out. People are probably just now showing up at The Pink Slipper."

Earlier, I relayed what Stan said about the case. For the first time, Dottie actually seemed impressed by how he makes his living.

"Let's talk about something else." Aunt Maeve puts the cap on the hair spray. "To take your mind off this."

"Nothing could do that."

Dottie comes around the counter and she and Aunt Maeve exchange nervous glances.

"Okay, what's up?"

"Daddy's coming."

"Daddy's—" I turn to Aunt Maeve.

"Your sister said she wanted to see him."

"Fine. But *I* don't want to see him."

"You don't have to, then," Dottie says. "You can lock yourself in the john with your head down the toilet for all I care."

"He's coming *here?* To my house?"

She nods.

Indignation rises up in me. I glance back and forth between the two of them. "You had no right to invite him."

Aunt Maeve sets down her comb. "I was hoping once he got here, you'd change your mind, honey."

"I won't change my mind. When is this little meeting supposed to take place?"

"In the morning."

"Tomorrow? Where is he that he can get here so fast?"

"At a motel close to downtown," Aunt Maeve answers. "He rode the bus in this afternoon. He wanted a good night's sleep before we get together."

I walk to the window and look out. "Did he say what he wants?"

"Just to talk to us," Dottie says quietly.

"Why?"

"I don't know. But I plan to find out."

I look back at Aunt Maeve. "Do you know?"

She shakes her head.

"Okay." I puff my cheeks, blow the air out slowly. "He can come here. I'll find something to do away from the house to keep me occupied while you visit. But I want him gone by six."

I see hope and anxiety in Dottie's eyes. "Maybe he's changed."

"His kind don't change," I snap. "Isn't that what you said about Dave because he left his family? How is Daddy any different, Dottie? Why are you so willing to forgive one and not the other?"

"It's not the same thing!" she yells at me, but I can see by her expression I've struck a chord and it rings true.

"Stop it!" Aunt Maeve jingles as she points a finger at us. "I won't stand by and listen to the two of you fight."

Dottie and I both cross our arms and glare at one another. "Fine," she finally says, sounding as exasperated with me as I am with her. "Back to Stanny's case, then, since Dinah's so hell-bent on worrying herself sick. I've been thinking about it." Walking to the table, she plucks the spiked red wig I've worn the past two nights off its stand and plops it onto her head. "I don't blame him one bit for not quitting the work he loves just to please you."

"*Dottie…*" Aunt Maeve's eyes narrow to slits and her voice holds a warning.

"Well, why would he?" Dottie tucks the ends of her hair beneath the wig. "He's on a stakeout right now. You have to admit that's a lot more exciting than selling rich snobs security systems."

"And a lot more dangerous," I add.

With the wig in place, she looks at me. "Remember what you told me about how you fell in love with him when he saved those people from the house fire? That's who he is. You fell in love with a cop. Why would you want to change him?"

I'm amazed to hear Dottie defending Stan. But I know she's right; take away his badge and he wouldn't be the man I fell in love with. Still, I can't help being afraid for him. And for myself. Our brief separation has reinforced how much my marriage means to me, how much *he* means.

"That wig looks good on you, cinnamon stick," Aunt Maeve says to Dottie in a none-too-subtle attempt to change the subject.

Dottie points at a chair and says to me, "For God's sake, sit down. You're making me nervous."

When I do sit, she twists my hair up and pins it. She lifts the dark wig that she's worn the past couple of nights from its stand. Tugging it onto my head, Dottie primps the curls with her fingers. "I can't believe that Lou Lou is Stanny's cousin." She laughs. "And to think we had the two of them doing the—"

"Please, Dottie," I interrupt. "I'd like to forget about that."

"So, Stan's partner is gonna pretend to be the guy from the chat room?"

"That's the plan."

"But Stan's the one who's really been talking to this Peter Pan guy, right?"

"Well, they both have, I think. Will's going to disguise himself to fit the description Stan gave Peter Pan."

"He should've had me fix his wig and makeup," Aunt Maeve says, setting aside the ash-blond flip and starting on an auburn shag.

Dottie comes around the chair to face me. She eyes her work, then tugs my wig a bit to the right. "So what do they think is the wacko's motive?"

"All the victims have met three criteria. They're gay, they cross-dress and they all have kids." I explain the rest of what the profiler told Stan.

"Sounds like one warped dude," Dottie says. "So he thinks he's avenging other kids with cross-dressing dads." She shakes her head. "I guess having children is a big issue for a lot of those guys."

I look up at her. "Why do you think that?"

"You know that waitress we were talking to the other night?"

"Which one? Josephine?"

"Josephine doesn't work there. I'm talking about the one in the poodle skirt. With the crooked teeth." She frowns. "Christy, I think."

"That's right. I tuned him out because I was watching Stan. What about him?"

"He said his old man liked to wear women's clothes, and that it was really hard on him when he was a kid. He thinks it's wrong for men who cross-dress to have children, and that—" Dottie presses her fingertips to her mouth and whispers, "Oh."

A chill rushes through me.

"Good God-a-mighty," Aunt Maeve murmurs.

Without a word, I stand and run into the bedroom for my purse. When I find my phone inside, I punch in Stan's cell number and get a message that his service is off. Holding the phone, I return to the kitchen, my heart thumping hard against my chest. "Stan's phone is off."

"What about Lou Lou?"

I find a phone book, look up the number for The Pink Slipper, punch it in while Dottie and Aunt Maeve hover around me.

After the fifth ring, someone picks up. "Pink Slipper," says a sandpaper voice. "Christy speaking."

I hang up, my heart jumping. "That was him!"

Dottie's eyes widen. "Christy?"

Nodding, I say, "I guess I should've asked for Stella but it freaked me out when I heard his voice."

"Call back."

Christy answers again. He says that Stella is tied up

and can't come to the phone. I pray that he doesn't mean that literally. Lou Lou, he explains, isn't in yet. I'm afraid to ask him to give Stan a message, even a seemingly harmless one. But I'm more afraid not to. "Would you have Stella call home, please?"

"Sure," he says, not sounding the least bit suspicious.

After I hang up, Dottie remembers one of Stan's e-mails had Lou Lou's cell phone number in it. We rush to the computer only to find that Stan had deleted the message.

Thirty minutes pass during which both Aunt Maeve and Dottie pace with me. Finally, I can't bear to wait anymore. "I'm going to The Pink Slipper."

Dottie looks grim. "I'm going with you."

"You stay here," I say to Aunt Maeve. "If Stan calls, tell him what's going on."

Her eyes darken with concern. "You girls be careful."

Dottie and I leave without taking the time to remove our wigs.

I feel light-headed as we weave our way through cars and trucks in The Pink Slipper's parking lot. A glance at my watch tells me it's nine-thirty. Will's meeting with the suspected kidnapper is scheduled for ten.

Midway through the lot, a man dressed in dark clothing and a baseball cap steps out from behind a pickup, blocking our path. In one quick movement, he lunges forward and grabs Dottie.

"I'll shoot if either of you so much as breathe," he says before I can scream. The man chuckles quietly as he glances at Dottie. "So you're Stella's wife."

Recognizing the gravelly voice as Christy's, I lift a hand and say, "No, you have—"

"Shut up!" he hisses, jabbing something hard into Dottie's side, making her gasp. "Not too smart, are you? Neither of you." He chuckles again and in a high voice says, "*Stan!*" mimicking my whimper when I recognized Stella. "Detective Hager. Well, well, well. He's gonna pop a vein when he finds out I've got you." Baring his crooked teeth, Christy eases Dottie toward the driver's side of the truck and snarls, "Get in."

Dottie does as he says, sliding across the seat when he climbs in beside her. Before the door slams, he looks at me and says, "Go tell Sergeant Hager I got his wife."

The engine turns over, and I stare in horror at the back of Dottie's head. Should I run toward them? Bang on the window? Scream? But I'm too paralyzed with fear to do any of those things. What if I did and he shot her?

Instead I memorize the license plate number as the truck pulls from the lot. Then, with my heart in my throat, I dash for The Pink Slipper's entrance.

CHAPTER 18

Inside The Pink Slipper rock music throbs as hard as the beat of my heart. The room is a smoky blur of color and movement. I push my way through, headed for the central bar, searching for Stan on the other side. I see his black ponytail before I see him. His head jerks up and his rouged face tenses when he notices me tearing across the room. His blank expression confuses me at first. Then, I remember that I'm wearing a different wig—Dottie's wig.

By the time I reach him, Stan recognizes me. He leans across the bar as I slam into it. "I thought I told you—"

"He's got Dottie," I gasp, tears streaking down my cheeks.

Glancing left to right, he murmurs, "Wait there." He steps back, says something to the other bartender then walks around to my side of the bar. Nonchalantly, he grasps my upper arm and guides me toward a door that leads to the back of the club. We push through.

"What's going on?" he asks in a quiet, intense voice as we hurry down a short hallway.

"Christy…he's Peter Pan. I tried to call you. Your phone is off, so we came. He grabbed Dottie in the parking lot."

"You could've called someone at the station when you couldn't reach me."

"I didn't think of it."

At the end of the hall, he unlocks a storage room. Inside, Ray Combs, another detective, faces a short, slim woman with auburn curls. Ray fumbles with the buttons on the front of the woman's green satin blouse. They both raise startled eyes when Stan and I burst in.

"Relax," Stan says. "It's Dinah."

Ray turns red, from his fleshy jowls to the top of his bald head. "Don't go calling Nancy on me, Dinah." Winking, he slides up a hand and squeezes the woman's right breast. "It's only Charmin."

Slapping his hand away, the woman meets my gaze and says, "It's me, Dinah. Will. Ray's wiring me."

Stan's partner makes a beautiful woman. I barely recognize the man beneath the makeup.

Will's eyes narrow on my face. I must look as frantic as I feel because he steps away from Ray and asks, "You okay?"

Turning to face Stan again, digging my fingers

into his arms, I sob, "Dottie and I changed wigs at the house…I—"

"Take a breath," Stan says.

"Christy knows who you are—that you're undercover—he's trying to get to you through me. He grabbed Dottie by mistake, thinking she's me."

"Jesus." Stan whisks a hand through his hair.

"They're in a black truck." I choke out the license plate number I memorized. "He's not dressed up tonight. He's wearing a dark ball cap and dark clothes. Dottie has on a short, red wig."

Stan springs into action and, suddenly, I'm invisible. "Got that?" he snaps, rushing toward Ray and Will.

Will dips his chin and talks into his right breast.

Ray lifts a two-way radio and barks orders.

Clutching my purse, I walk to the opposite side of the room. My cell phone vibrates inside my purse at the same time Ray says, "Mikey's on him, he saw the truck leave the lot headed north."

Across the room, Stan punches numbers on his cell phone as I pull mine from my purse and press it to my ear. "Hello?"

My breath catches as Christy's gruff voice travels across the connection. "Don't flinch or make a sound or your sister's toast. Say 'yes' if you understand me."

"Yes." I struggle to keep my voice steady.

"Are you with Hager? 'Yes' or 'no'?"

"Yes."

"I have a gun to your sister's head. Pretend you're talking to that kooky aunt of yours."

His low chuckle sends a chill up my spine as I realize that, sometime between last night and today, he researched my family. I draw a deep breath to steady my nerves. Pull myself together. For Dottie's sake. For the baby. What would I do if he hurt them? Pressing a hand to my opposite ear, I walk farther away from the others in the room, as if distancing myself from them in order to hear the phone call. "Okay, Aunt Maeve," I say.

"That's good," Christy murmurs. "Keep talking and nodding. Looks like I grabbed the wrong girl. Let's fix that, okay?"

"Yes. Okay."

"Pretend you broke the connection, but don't. Then excuse yourself to go to the can."

Returning the phone to my purse, I cross to Stan. After he ends his call, I say, "I feel sick. I need to go to the rest room."

He nods Will over. "Walk Dinah to the bathroom. Then we'll proceed with the previous plan. Just in case, by some weird coincidence, Christy's not Peter Pan, and we've got two crazies on our hands."

Will and I slip out front and he walks me to the

ladies' room. "I'll be sitting right over there at the bar waiting on my date," he says into my ear. "I'll keep an eye on the door."

Thanking him, I go inside and turn the lock. I pull my phone from my purse. "I'm alone," I say quietly into it.

"Good," Christy says. "We're gonna have a little trade-off. You for your sister."

As Christy gives me directions to a deserted warehouse northwest of town, I wage an inner debate. Should I trust him to let Dottie go if I follow his instructions? Or should I hang up and go straight to Stan?

The choice is obvious. Stan is the one I should trust; he'll know what to do.

As I reach for the doorknob, Christy says, "Don't even think about tipping off your husband or his friends."

I drop my hand to my side.

"Keep your mouth shut if you ever want to see your sister alive again. Am I clear?"

"Yes. Don't hurt her. Please."

"It's up to you." He breaks the connection.

When I exit the rest room, I see Stan behind the bar. Will sits across from him, an empty stool beside him. I cross to them. "I think I—" Dizzy with fear, I pause to catch my breath.

Tell him.

I reach for the bar to steady myself. "I—"

It's up to you.

"I want to go home to Aunt Maeve. She should know what's going on."

Stan looks around to make sure no one is listening then says, "Stay there until you hear from me. I'll get Dottie back unharmed. I promise."

Pressing my lips together tightly, I nod at him.

Stan nods back then says, "Someone will be watching to make sure you get safely to your car."

Aware that he's already spoken to the officers staked outside the club and instructed them to keep an eye on me, I make my way toward the door.

My mind races. Christy won't make the trade; I know that. But what if I told Stan the truth, and Dottie died because of my decision? Then again, what if she died because I *didn't* tell him?

I want to scream, pound the walls, rewind this night, start over and do everything differently. Then Stan's voice breaks through the chaos in my mind. *You have to trust me.*

Trust. Why is that so hard for me to do? I should turn around. Run to him. Let him take over. It's his job. His expertise.

I start to turn…

Keep your mouth shut if you ever want to see your sister alive again.

Dizzy with fear and uncertainty, I open the door and step out, let it close behind me. The music inside muffles, replaced by the sound of cars on the streets. A shiver ripples across my skin, despite the warm summer air. Gravel crunches beneath my shoe as I step off the concrete porch into the parking lot. I pause, close my eyes, and see Dottie's face, the plea in her expression.

I need you.

My sister has always needed me. She needs me now.

But until this moment, I never realized how much I need her, too.

My pulse thumps hard and fast as the city's lights recede in my rearview mirror. I shift my focus to the dark stretch of highway ahead, illuminated by the car's headlights. Off to my right in the distance, I spot an exit onto a dirt road. I squint to read the sign, hoping it's the farm-to-market road Christy instructed me to turn down. A shaky breath shudders out of me when I see that it is.

Inside the purse propped against my leg, my cell phone vibrates, making me jump.

"Someone's calling," I say. "My phone just went off. What should I do?"

"Answer it," comes Stan's reply from the backseat.

Will, who is driving the Accord and wearing my wig since he's closer to my size, glances across to where I sit in the passenger seat. "Take a deep breath," he says. "You're gonna do fine."

Swallowing my apprehension, I reach inside my purse for the phone.

I was relieved, nervous and surprised all at once when Stan and his partner agreed to let me go along, to take part in Dottie's rescue. Oh, it took some talking on my part to convince them my plan could work; don't get me wrong. Stan was afraid to "have me underfoot," he said. But I could see that he was more afraid that I'd get hurt. He wanted me to go home and wait, let him and his partners figure out how to bring in Christy without risking Dottie. Uncertainty that I could be counted on to do that probably played into his change of heart. Considering my behavior lately, I can understand that. Whatever the case, in the end, we compromised. Now, I'm wired and ready, literally and emotionally. There's no turning back.

I push the talk button, press the phone to my ear.

"What's keeping you?"

It's Christy. I catch my breath. "I just turned off the highway. I shouldn't be long now."

"You've got ten minutes."

"Is my sister okay? Let me talk to her. How do I know you haven't already..." I can't bring myself to finish that thought.

"Dinah?"

I gasp. "Dottie! Oh, God—"

"I'm okay. Don't—"

"Quiet, bitch," Christy hisses, and I hear a sharp intake of breath and cringe, afraid that he's hurting her.

"If you harm my—"

"Ten minutes. And you better show up alone. Park in back and step out of the car with your hands over your head."

"Then what?"

"Don't you worry about that. I'll tell you what to do." He breaks the connection.

I end the call, lower the phone to my lap and repeat Christy's instructions to Stan and Will.

They converse back and forth, then Stan gives orders to his backup team over a handset.

"I know this place," he says after a few seconds. "It's around the next turn. We've got more than enough time. Pull over."

"What are you doing?" I ask, panicked when Stan opens the back door.

"I get off here." He climbs out then looks in at me

and winks. "Don't worry, sweetheart. I'll be right there with you. You just won't see me." He taps his ear. "Just listen to Will and me. You'll do fine."

The door closes. Will rolls down all the windows and takes off. "Get on the floorboard," he says. After I do, he continues, "Here's how it'll go down. I'll step out of the car, like I'm you, and stand beside the driver's side door." He glances down at me. "After I'm out, you think you can ease over here close to my window without being seen or hitting the horn?"

"Believe me, I'll be careful."

"That's my girl." He smiles. "Keep your face close to the window. Close to me. Stan will be talking in your ear. He'll tell you what to say. Say it loud enough so that asshole will hear it."

"Stan will be close enough to know what's going on?"

"Trust me, he already is."

I close my eyes and take several deep breaths.

"Here we are," Will murmurs as the car slows to a stop. He puts it in park, cuts the lights and the engine. With one last tug at his wig, he opens the door and whispers, "Showtime."

When the door closes, I ease my way over into the driver's seat. From my crouched position, I can see him outside the window, his hands overhead, a gun tucked into the waistband of his skirt.

"I can't see your hands," a deep voice calls out from somewhere beyond the front of the car.

Will raises his arms higher.

I peek over the dash and catch a glimpse of two figures, one in front of the other. The first one looks to be a woman with her hands behind her back, something tied around her eyes. *Oh, Dottie, no,* I think as a beam of light bursts through the darkness toward the car, limiting my vision.

"Don't look away," Christy bellows.

"Tell him the flashlight's blinding you," Stan murmurs quietly in my ear.

"The light," I yell. "You're blinding me!"

"Do what I say or I'll kill your sister and her baby."

"Dottie, are you okay?" I call, without any instruction from Stan.

I hear her cry out, then Christy growls, "I'll tell you when you can talk." His voice seems to move closer. "You alone?"

"Yes." I shrink down into the floorboard as light floods the front window, moves from side to side, then away.

"Drop your keys on the ground."

A soft jingle of metal. I ease up toward the side window again.

"Step into the light."

"Don't say anything," Stan murmurs in my ear.

"I said step into the light!"

"Let her go first," I call out at Stan's instruction.

And then Christy laughs, and the sound of it raises the fine hairs on the nape of my neck. "I don't think so," he says. "*First*, the three of us will have a little fun."

A guttural wail shatters the silence. A primal sound. A mother bear protecting her young. There's a thud. Christy's cry. One gunshot. Then another and another. Voices shouting. Footsteps pounding the dirt.

Adrenaline and fear propel me up into the seat. My heart beats so loudly it drowns out the sound of everything else. I hit the headlights, see Dottie on the ground, a man sprawled beside her, blood on both of them.

In a blink, cops are everywhere, and I'm out of the car without realizing I ever opened the door. Strong arms hold me back. I taste salty tears on my lips, the metallic taste of terror. "Dottie!" I scream as Stan crouches beside her. He tugs a dingy blindfold off of her as I break free of the officer holding me and stumble toward them.

I drop to my knees in the dirt in time to hear Dottie whisper, "Stanny." She shifts to look at me, smiles. Then her eyes flutter and close.

CHAPTER 19

We gather in the emergency-room waiting area, Stan and Lou Lou, Aunt Maeve and me. Aunt Maeve sits quietly with her eyes closed while Lou Lou holds her hand. They only met an hour ago, but connected immediately. I wonder if, in the other they each saw a kindred spirit, another soul out of sync with society's accepted rhythm.

From the corner where he stands, Stan watches me pace. "The bullet only grazed her leg. She'll be okay," he says.

Once I realized Dottie wasn't mortally wounded, I tucked in my emotions, smoothed them tight for her sake. But now they unravel again. "I was so scared I'd lost them. Both of them," I choke through a sob. "What was she thinking tearing into Christy like that when he had a gun on her?" But I already know the answer; she thought it was the only chance of saving the baby, herself and me. She didn't know Will was the one outside the car wearing my wig. Or that Stan hid in the shadows with an entire SWAT team to back him up.

Stan pushes away from the wall, comes over and wraps me in his arms. "Your sister's either very brave or very foolish."

"Both," I murmur, sinking into his warm, solid comfort. "What will happen to Christy?"

"After they dig my bullet out of his shoulder, he better hope he looks good in orange. If he'd shot an inch lower, he might've killed Will."

Behind Stan, I see Dave Reno push through the doors from outside. He looks in bad need of a smoke. When he sees my face, his turns ashen and he stops in his tracks.

Stepping from Stan's embrace, I say, "As far as we know, she's okay. The doctor should be out soon."

I hear the relieved shudder of his sigh. "What about the baby?"

"I don't know."

Dave pinches the bridge of his nose. "If anything happens…"

Stan moves up beside me. I glance at him, then go to Dave. We cling to each other.

"I've done some stupid things in my life," he says, "but the worst was pissing her off."

"You really love her?"

"More than anything."

As much as my sister means to me, seeing the way she treats Dave, I'm at a loss as to why he'd be so crazy about her. I'm through playing guessing games, tiptoeing around my questions. A baby's future is at stake. "She's said some harsh things about you," I say, easing back to look at him.

"That's just Dottie's way of trying to convince herself she doesn't love me. I got too close, and that scares the hell out of her." His laugh is humorless. "Then, like an idiot, I gave her an ultimatum, thinking she'd be forced to admit she needed me. Either we got married or I hit the road. Christ, I know her better than to do a dipshit thing like that. Nobody manipulates Dottie. It was the excuse she needed to walk away."

As much as I don't want to, I like the man. It's obvious he knows Dottie inside and out, backward and forward. Her weaknesses, her fears, what makes her tick. A man doesn't look that deeply into a woman unless he really cares.

"I want to do things right this time around," Dave continues. "Be more than just a part-time dad. My girls and I only saw each other three or four times a year while they were growing up—that's not enough."

"Dottie said you've done time," Stan says.

Huffing, he shakes his head. "That's my Dottie.

Trying to get all of you on her side against me. I did a stint in juvy when I was a kid after a couple of buddies and me took a joyride in a stranger's car."

The doors leading back to the examining rooms push open and a doctor walks through. "Anyone here with Dottie Dewberry?"

Aunt Maeve opens her eyes and she and Lou Lou join us.

The young resident scans our little group, his gaze traveling down the line: Lou Lou in his pink sequined evening gown; Aunt Maeve in her gypsy garb; Dave looking like a middle-aged mafia hit man; Stan still in his women's clothing and makeup, though the wig is off. My wig is off, too, and my hair is an every-which-way mess.

"How is she?" I ask.

"She has a slight flesh wound, right thigh, and a broken wrist." He mumbles some medical mumbo jumbo but all I hear are the words, "She'll be fine."

Before I can speak, Dave asks, "And the baby?"

"He's fine, too." The doctor smiles. "I'd like to keep Miss Dewberry overnight, though. Just as a precaution."

Relief sweeps through me. "Can we see her?"

"She's asking for Mr. Reno." The doctor glances between Dave and Stan. Then Dave moves toward him, and he nods. "After you visit with her, we'll get her moved to a room upstairs and you can all peek in on her."

"Thank the stars," Aunt Maeve says quietly as Dave follows the doctor through the swinging doors.

"Anyone for coffee?" Lou Lou asks. "I'll make a run."

Stan and I decline.

"I'll go with you," Aunt Maeve says.

Lou Lou's high heels click against the hard floor tiles and Aunt Maeve's bracelets jingle as they walk away, side by side.

"I still can't get used to seeing Lawrence like that," Stan says, watching them go.

I study his baffled expression and try not to laugh. "But you're okay with it now, right?"

"Okay with it?" Scratching his head, he looks at me. "Let's just say I accept it and leave it at that."

"I hated him when I thought the two of you—"

Stan stops my words with an upraised hand. "Don't go there, okay?"

I grin. "He seems like a very nice man."

"He is." Stan glances toward the doorway again. "The guy throws a mean left hook."

"Lou Lou?"

"He used to whip my ass on a regular basis when we were kids."

I laugh at the image that conjures.

Stan's cheek twitches as he leads me to the connected row of hard plastic chairs where I left my purse. I move the purse to the floor so I can sit, and it tips over. A baby rattle tumbles out. It came with some of the clothes Aunt Maeve and I bought, and I put it in my purse because it made me smile every time I reached for my keys or cell phone. It does now, too, as I pick it up. "Dottie..." I smile and shake my head. "She wanted me to think Dave's a criminal so I wouldn't warm to him. So I'd be worried about the kind of men she chooses, and go through with the adoption."

Stan watches me closely. "I have a good feeling about Dave."

"Me, too."

"How do you feel about that?"

"Torn."

He takes the rattle from my hand. "I've been thinking about the adoption. If that's what you and Dottie want, I'm good with it."

I stare at my knees. "I'm pretty sure I'm about to be an aunt instead of a mother." Shrugging, I manage a smile. "I've never been an aunt. I'm excited about it."

He dips his chin until I look him in the eye. "Are you?"

"Yes."

When he gives the rattle back to me, his hand remains on mine. "I want to keep trying," he says. "See another doctor. Maybe go to Dallas and see someone there. Or we could adopt a different baby, if you want." Clearing his throat, he adds, "And now that this case is solved, I'm ready to go into business with Pete. I've had enough excitement to last me a while."

"No." I shake my head. "You're a cop. It's who you are. I don't want you to give it up for me. I couldn't live with that. And as for having a baby…I want one, but if it doesn't happen, I'll be okay." We both glance toward the hallway as Lou Lou and Aunt Maeve approach carrying coffee cups and cackling. "Our life is full of family all of a sudden, wouldn't you say? Not that there won't always be room for one more. But ours looks pretty complete to me right now, as is."

It makes me sad that it took Christy threatening Aunt Maeve, Dottie and the baby, for me to realize exactly how important they are to me. And for Stan to realize the same thing about his cousin.

Aunt Maeve and Lou Lou glance at us, whisper to each other, then take seats on the far side of the room. Lou Lou holds out a hand for Aunt Maeve's inspection, and I hear mention of a cuticle treatment.

"You think Dottie will marry Dave?" Stan asks.

"Who knows? Eventually, I guess. I'm sure she loves him, she's just paranoid. It's like she's waiting for him to prove something."

"Until he does that, she can stay with us. The baby, too."

"Thanks. I'll tell her. It would only be temporary. Until she gets on her feet." I look at him, smile. "My sister's not so bad once you get used to her. She'll grow on you."

"Like a wart?" he asks, but his eyes are teasing. "With this crazy crew we've acquired," he adds, "I almost wish I could see into the future. To brace myself for whatever's ahead."

"I know just the person to help you with that." I catch Aunt Maeve's attention and call her and Lou Lou over to join us. "How's the coffee?" I ask when they sit down.

"It's tea," Aunt Maeve says.

"I thought it might be." I nod toward Stan. "Now that this is all over, he's wondering what lies ahead."

Aunt Maeve looks pleased and a tad surprised by my unspoken suggestion. Then her eyes take on a familiar faraway look. Lifting the soggy tea bag, she hands it to Stan then holds the foam cup of hot water in front of him. "Break the bag into the water," she says in her sultry, hushed tea-reader voice. "I don't think I've ever read your leaves before, have I?"

* * *

Dottie is dressed and watching television early the next morning when I arrive at the hospital to take her home. We didn't get to talk much last night. She was too sleepy and there were too many people in the room.

"Hi," she says now when I walk in. "Get me the hell out of here."

"Soon," I say. "I just talked to the nurse. They're bringing a wheelchair."

"I don't need one."

"Hospital policy." I sit at the edge of the bed. "How're you feeling?"

"Lucky."

"That was a gutsy thing you did. Stupid, too. You could've been killed."

"I thought it was you outside the car. He had me blindfolded."

"Even if you could've seen, you probably would've thought it was me. It was dark, and Will had on my wig."

"That's what I hear." She sighs. "I knew that bastard wasn't about to let me go. It wouldn't have mattered if he did, anyway. I couldn't have left you."

Her gaze drifts to the television. I look, too. "What are you watching?"

"*American Graffiti,*" she says, her voice softening. "I couldn't believe it when I flipped the channel and there it was. I have it on video. Must've watched it a hundred times, at least. It was filmed in '73 or '74."

Not long after our mother left. I glance at Dottie, then quickly back at the screen. We watch in silence for a minute.

"Look…here's the part," she says, pushing up to sit straighter in the bed. "See that woman? There…in the background, with the light brown hair."

Though I see the actress she points out, I don't say anything.

"That could be her, don't you think?"

I don't need to ask who she's talking about.

The scene shifts, and the actress disappears. Dottie sinks back against the pillows, reaches for the remote and turns the television off. "We didn't hold on tight enough to her, did we? Daddy, either," she says quietly.

"We held on." I still do. To every bad memory. To the pain they left behind. To my bitterness toward them. "They're the ones who didn't hold on tight enough to us." When she doesn't respond, I swallow, then say, "I'm sorry we fought. You know, before we went to The Pink Slipper last night. I'm sorry for the other times, too, and the things I've said."

"Dinah, I've said some—"

"No, let me talk." I take a long breath, then another. "You'll make a wonderful mother, Dottie.

You're full of love. It bubbles out of you. I admire that about you. The way you don't hold back what you're feeling, good or bad. I wish I could be that way." My chest aches, and I'm afraid I'm going to cry. "I don't think I've ever told you how much you've always meant to me. When we were kids, I would've been so alone without you."

"You had to grow up too fast." She blinks misty eyes. "For both of us."

"That wasn't your fault. We were thrown away like yesterday's newspaper, and we handled it in different ways."

"I don't know, Di. At least Daddy—" She blinks at me. "I think he did the right thing by taking us to Aunt Maeve. I'm glad he did it."

For the first time, I try to consider what Daddy did from his perspective at the time—that of a down-on-his-luck, heartbroken twenty-seven-year-old man with a missing wife and two young daughters. The truth in Dottie's statement settles into me, but there's still so much about his choices that I don't understand. So much that still stings. "He could've stayed in Coopersville. Or at least visited on holidays. More than that."

"I know," Dottie whispers. "I don't get that, either. I hope he can explain. Will you stay at the house when he comes by later today?"

I nod and take her hand. "I'm so glad I had you back then. I know sometimes I made you feel like I was ashamed of—"

She squeezes my fingers. "You don't have to do this."

"No, I do. I *was* ashamed sometimes. I hate it, but it's true. I took my anger at Mama and Daddy out on you and Aunt Maeve. But it was really them I was ashamed of."

"Come here," Dottie says in a choked whisper.

I lean over and hug her, careful of her arm in the cast. "That's one very lucky little boy you're carrying. He has quite a mother."

We pull apart. Dottie presses her lips together, her eyes filling again. "I can't give him up," she whispers. "Not even to you. I'm sorry."

"I know that, honey. I don't want you to. But, oh am I ever going to spoil that little guy."

We both laugh.

"Stan and I were talking," I tell her. "I don't know what the situation is between you and Dave, but you and the baby have a place with us if you need it, until you're on your feet."

"I appreciate that. Could I let you know?"

"Sure." I watch her a few seconds in silence. "Dave loves you. You know that, don't you?"

"I love him."

"Then what's the problem?"

She looks down at her stomach. "Why didn't he put up a fight about signing those legal papers relinquishing his rights?"

"You were going to sign, too," I remind her.

"Because I thought it was for the best, not because someone told me to do it." She frowns and lifts her chin. "Aren't me and his baby worth fighting for?"

I hear a noise outside the door and, when I look over, the nurse pushes a wheelchair across the threshold. Dave follows, carrying a bouquet of red roses.

The hope and love in his eyes bring tears to mine. Looking back at Dottie, I smile. "People fight in different ways, Dot," I tell her, then stand so Dave can take my place at her side.

CHAPTER 20

Dottie

Hey, Peep. I guess I'll quit calling you that now. Your daddy and I decided to name you William Stanley. William, after Will, the cop who took a bullet in the shoulder to save our butts. Stanley, after your uncle Stan, who shot Christy. And, speaking of your uncle Stan, as it turns out, he's an okay guy. He's coming around, though he could still stand to lighten up a little; I'll work on that.

I love you so much, Peep. I know I've never told you, but it's true. It's my love for you that made me think I had to give you up. You deserve a better mother than the one I had. And I've always been so afraid I'm cut from her mold. Afraid that her genes in me form some sort of road map I can't help but follow.

But no matter how much I'm like her, there's

a part of me that isn't. I know that now, because last night when your life was in danger, the thought of losing you was more than I could stand. I won't ever hurt you like Mama hurt me and Dinah. That's a promise. I will never do anything to make you feel you're less than the precious miracle you are. Nothing means more to me than you. Nothing.

I felt lost all those years that Dinah and I were apart. And I'd be lost without you, too. That's how I'm different than Mama. That's how I know we belong together, you and me. You're mine. I'll do my best at being your mom. I'll never let you go.

We won't be going back to Vegas. Your daddy plans to look for work here so you can grow up around family. Besides playing piano, he has experience as a mechanic. And, years back, he drove a beer delivery truck. Oh, and for a while he worked as a dog groomer. We have a love of dogs in common. Maybe we could go into business together.

Anyway, we're going to find ourselves a little house with a yard. I'm going to put up that wallpaper border in your bedroom. The one with the sailboats. Maybe we'll have a patio in back with a barbecue grill. And we could put a basketball goal beside the driveway for when you're older. What the hell, I might even decide to fly a flag out front. The idea of all that is starting to grow on me....

CHAPTER 21

Dinah

Last night, Aunt Maeve called Daddy and postponed his coming over until noon, since Dottie was staying overnight in the hospital. While she goes to pick him up at his motel, Stan slices cantaloupe and I fix chicken salad sandwiches. Dottie, Dave and Lou Lou sit at the kitchen counter and talk to us. Hoot and Saxon hover protectively at Dottie's feet.

"It's *fabulous*," Lou Lou exclaims, eyeing the small sparkling diamond on Dottie's left hand.

Along with the roses, Dave gave her the engagement ring before we left the hospital. While the nurse and I looked on, he dropped to his knees on the cold hard floor beside Dottie's bed and proposed.

"And your answer was?" Lou Lou asks, then bites his lower lip and presses a hand to his chest.

Dottie throws her uncasted arm around Dave. "Yes," she says, beaming, though her voice sounds stunned.

Lou Lou claps his hands, now adorned with a new set of fiberglass nails Aunt Maeve applied last night.

I laugh. "After that, Dave was the one that needed to be pushed out to the car in a wheelchair, not Dottie."

"I still can't figure out what I did right this time," Dave says, chuckling and holding Dottie.

When the laughter stops, Lou Lou asks, "Are you sure you want me here when your father arrives? This is a family affair."

"You are family," I say.

Lou Lou looks at Stan, his heavily-lined eyes full of uncertainty.

"Your ass stays put, Lawrence," Stan says. "You're not getting out of this that easy. From now on, our family sticks together through the good times *and* the tough ones."

Lou Lou looks pleased. "I hope your father has an open mind sweeties," he says to Dottie and me.

"He's not in any position to have an opinion," I mumble.

Dottie props her casted arm on the counter. "Tell me if I made this up, Dinah."

I cut a sandwich in half. "What?"

"Dancing on Daddy's feet when we were little. You know, holding his hands and standing on top of his feet while he moved to some kind of fast, funny music."

The memory jars me, and I feel dizzy and strange. I hear the tune in my mind, hear Daddy's deep laughter, feel his big hands clasping my fingers and his feet shuffling beneath mine, holding me up, sashaying me around the room to the song's beat.

"I'd forgotten about that." My voice sounds faraway.

I made a point to forget *all* the nice memories of him. They were too painful. Or maybe I just didn't want to be reminded that, despite Daddy's many faults, once there was goodness in his soul. Love of life. Love for us.

"He and Mama had an old turntable and a stack of forty-fives," I say.

"So it *was* real!" Dottie laughs. "What was that song?"

I hum a few bars. "No, that's wrong." I try again. then sing. "Charlie Brown, Charlie Brown, he's a clown, that Charlie Brown. He's gonna get caught, just you wait and see…Why's everybody always pickin' on me?"

Dottie laughs again. "That's it! And he'd dip us low on the last part."

My breath comes too fast now, too shallow. Glancing across at Stan, I find him watching me, his eyes gentle and aware. My hand shakes as I lift the knife. It slips from my fingers and clatters against the counter.

No one seems to notice but Stan. He picks up the knife and slices the next sandwich as Dave and Lou Lou listen raptly to Dottie. More details of our shared memory come back to her, and she relays them with delight in her voice.

Walking to the sink, I turn my back on them, twist on the faucet and look out the window. But instead of my yard, I see a different one, a bigger one with a driveway beside it and an oak tree rather than a mulberry. There's a small yellow bike with training wheels on the sidewalk, a pink bike with a banana seat lying beside it. Daddy stands in the grass. Dark wavy hair, tanned arms beneath Dottie's, lifting her up, twirling her 'round and 'round as she squeals. Daddy's voice calling…

"Your turn, Di."

"I'm too big for that, Daddy."

His eyes smiling down at me, dark and adoring. Those strong tanned arms lowering Dottie to the grass then scooping me up. *"Not yet, Baby Doll. You're still my little girl."*

"You okay?" Stan asks quietly, his hands on my shoulders.

With a nod, I exhale, trembling.

What will he look like? What will he say? Why did he want this meeting? To apologize? To give us some news? To try to become a part of our lives again now that he's old and alone? Is he sick? Does he need money?

A part of me hopes for a miracle. Words spoken by my father that will erase the last thirty-three years, words that will make me understand and forgive. A fairy-tale ending to three decades of bitterness and re-sentment and self-doubt. But what could he say? You're still my little girl? Would that make it better?

At five after twelve, I hear a car engine outside of the house. Everyone stops talking. I don't dare look at Dottie for fear we'll both crumble. I feel as if I'm caught in an undertow, sand shifting beneath my feet, the breath sucked from my lungs.

The front door rattles, clicks shut. Aunt Maeve walks into the kitchen. Alone.

Her face is pale. Her eyes too bright. She clears her throat. "Al can't bring himself to come in. He's out in the car."

I stare at her a moment, then look away. "So what are we supposed to do?"

"Halfway here, he wanted me to take him back to the motel and give you this afterward, but I wouldn't do it." Aunt Maeve reaches into her big suede purse and pulls out a folded envelope. Her hand is shaking. "He said he wrote it in case y'all changed your mind about the visit."

"*He's* the coward," I snap. "Here we've been nervous wrecks waiting on him, making him lunch, psyching ourselves up for whatever it is he thinks he needs to say, and he backs out just like that?"

"I told him I'd let the two of you read his letter and

then you could decide whether or not he should come in." Aunt Maeve holds the envelope out to me.

When I don't take it, Stan says, "You want me to read it, Dinah?"

I cross my arms. "I couldn't care less what the man wrote." How dare he put everyone here in such an awkward position? Lou Lou looks as if he has changed his mind about joining this tense, screwed-up family and, though Dave wraps an arm around Dottie's shoulder, he looks cornered, too.

When I see that Dottie's on the verge of tears, I snatch the envelope from Aunt Maeve's outstretched hand. I don't know why Dottie's so emotional. The man's not worth the effort it takes to avoid crying. Besides, I'm not surprised that he wants to run away. The bigger surprise would've been if he didn't.

I unfold the envelope. Coffee stains one corner. Words are scribbled in blue ink across it in cursive letters, tiny and tight.

First, I read the note through silently, then back up and read it aloud, my voice as flat as the bread we've been slicing.

Girls,

  If you're reading this, you decided not to see me.
That's okay. I understand if you don't want to. I

thought I should tell you of your mother's passing from lung cancer in March. She's buried in Flagstaff, Arizona. I've kept in touch with her cousin Jean through Christmas cards over the years. When Jean had news of Patsy, she'd tell me. I never told you, because I wasn't sure you'd want to hear. But I thought you'd want to know she died. Your mama remarried late in life. Before that, I tried to visit her a few times. Two or three of those when she was in one mental ward or another, but she wouldn't see me. She never had no more children. Only you. She never did make an actress. Patsy retired as a salesclerk from JCPenney. A shame all she missed for that. A shame all I missed.

Maeve says I have a grandson on the way. That's a fine thing. I really wanted to see you girls, but even with the best intentions sometimes things don't work out like you plan. If you ever change your mind and want to get together, I'll come back quick as a whistle. I promise.

Dad

I hear Dottie sniffling as I stare at the envelope. Mama's dead. Why can't I cry about that? I only feel a numb sadness that our chance of ever seeing her again has slipped away. Still, I'm relieved in a way.

Dottie can quit searching for a glimpse of Patsy Dewberry's face in every movie she watches.

"I'm so sorry about your mother," Lou Lou murmurs. "You poor things."

When I look up, Dottie is swiping at her eyes. "I never knew her. I guess that makes me more sad than the fact that she died."

I look down at the pinched handwriting again. *I'll come back quick as a whistle. I promise.* Daddy's same old line. His same old lie.

Stepping to the counter, I hand the envelope to Dottie.

She reads through it again silently, the space between her brows puckered, her face as white as Aunt Maeve's. "How does he seem?" she asks in a small voice when she finishes.

"Nervous." Aunt Maeve sounds choked. "Afraid and lonely." Averting her gaze, she whispers, "Lost."

"We didn't get a chance to see Mama again," Dottie says, her wide eyes pleading with me, "but we can still see him. Why don't we hear him out? What could it hurt?"

Taking a deep breath, I walk toward the counter. "Let's go," I say. "We don't have anything to cower about."

She stands and meets me in the center of the kitchen. Holding hands, we walk to the door.

He doesn't see us step onto the porch. Smoking a cigarette and looking down at the sidewalk, Daddy paces in front of Aunt Maeve's purple Beetle. I say it's Daddy—I don't recognize the man with thinning gray hair and a stooped body so gaunt his shirt and slacks hang off it as if it's a wire coat hanger. He drops the cigarette, crushes it with the heel of his shoe, takes another step, hesitates and backs up. Crouching, he picks up the butt and quickly uses his fingers to sweep at the spot on the sidewalk where it fell.

"*Oh,*" Dottie cries. One anguished word that sums up how broken he looks, how desperate.

The stranger on the sidewalk goes still, turns his head and squints up at us.

Deep grooves across his forehead, along his sunken cheeks. Sallow skin. Thin lips.

The face is old and tired and unfamiliar. But I know the eyes. They're the same eyes I see in the mirror each morning, only wearier, hopeless, defeated. Afraid. Still, I recognize them as the eyes in my memories that once danced with life and purpose. That showered me with love.

How many times have I hoped that he suffered? My wish came true; the proof stands before me. Why don't

I feel gratified? Appeased? Instead, my chest aches and the same distress I heard in Dottie's cry clogs my throat. I feel as though I've fallen off the earth and I'm tumbling through space at a dizzying speed.

Then Dottie's fingers press into my palm. I squeeze her hand. She pulls me back.

Together, we leave the porch and start down the walkway toward our father.

Long before dawn the next morning, I'm awake, listening to the howl of a West Texas wind outside, the beginning of a summer storm. Again and again, I replay yesterday in my mind.

In the end, neither Dottie nor I brought ourselves to bring up the past, to ask him questions. We ate an awkward lunch and, later, a slightly less awkward dinner, growing a bit more relaxed together as the hours passed. We talked about the ordeal with Christy, about Dottie's baby, about our work. He told us about places he'd been, sights he'd seen, jobs he'd worked—construction, mostly, tending bar at a dive or two. Lou Lou jokingly offered him a job at The Slipper. He laughed, was polite, but remained distant with Stan's cousin all afternoon and evening, never quite meeting Lou Lou's eyes when they spoke. Not that he met any of our eyes; he seemed to have a hard time with that.

Aunt Maeve never left his side. Even while trying different wigs on Lou Lou, she made sure he sat next to her. She and Daddy spent hours laughing over times from their childhood, never mentioning Mama in those memories, though I know she was a part of them all.

I listened and watched him warily, careful not to seem eager to accept any kindness from him—a polite word, a smile, a compliment. Stingy with what I gave back in return. Reluctant to let go of my resentment. Still, we shared the same room, two meals at the same table, polite conversation. All things I never thought we'd do.

At times, I'd glance up and find him studying my face, or Dottie's with a sorrowful expression. But he'd look away quickly, flushing and nervous, when he realized he'd been caught.

It was close to midnight before Lou Lou left wearing an auburn shag Aunt Maeve loaned him. Dave followed a few minutes later.

Because of the hour, Dottie asked Daddy to stay the night. We'd made plans to drive out to Palo Duro Canyon State Park for a picnic in the morning. He'd loved the canyon growing up, and wanted to see it again. No sense in someone having to drive downtown to pick him up, Dottie said.

Her invitation startled me. Him, too, judging from

the look on his face. Still I found myself agreeing he should stay. To my surprise, he did, though it was apparent he felt awkward when the time came for me to make up the couch for him.

Now, at the foot of the bed, Saxon stirs and whines; my cue to let him out to do his business. He follows me through the dark house and slips into the backyard when I open the door. The wind is cool and it isn't raining yet, so I decide to leave him out for a while.

On my way back to bed, I hear a noise at the front of the house. Turning, I creep through the living room toward the kitchen, careful not to wake Daddy on the couch, squinting in that direction as I pass by. In the moonlight from the window, I see that the couch is empty, the linens and blanket neatly folded and stacked on the center cushion with the pillow on top. I walk over, find a photograph lying on the pillow. I switch on the lamp.

The picture is of Dottie and me with Mama and Daddy. Dottie looks to be two years old, which would make me four. Mama holds Dottie in her lap; Daddy holds me. We're all touching, the four of us; hand-to-hand, shoulder-to-shoulder, hip-to-hip. All smiling. Real smiles, not posed for the camera. Happiness shines from our eyes.

I'm light-headed, uneasy, as I move to the front

window, push open the shutters and look out, knowing what I'll see.

He stands on the sidewalk in profile, gazing down the street, his shoulders slumped against the wind. I reach through the slats and touch the glass with my fingertips. A cab pulls to the curb, the light on top illuminating the darkness with the word *taxi*.

"I never got around to asking him my questions," Dottie says quietly from behind me.

I glance back at her, pass her the photo then return my attention to the window in time to see Daddy open the cab door. "You mean why he left us?"

"Yes. And why he never came back."

"You know why. He was looking for her. You searched in movies. He searched in town after town."

"But she's gone now. Why can't he stay?"

"I don't know, Dottie. Maybe we bring back too many things that he can't bear to face."

Daddy starts to climb into the cab, then pauses. With one hand on the door, he looks back at the house. And, just like that, my resentment dissolves like sugar in hot water, leaving behind only pity and sorrow. What he wrote on the envelope is true. It is a shame what Mama missed. What *he* missed. What he's missing still. He'll probably never know Dottie's son. He never knew his own children, not really; only the babies in the photo. He's alone in the world, with no family and not much of a life, perfect or otherwise. Dottie and I faced the demons in our pasts, battled them to find our way back to each other, so we could move on. I guess Daddy doesn't have the strength to do that now. If he ever did.

I'll never forget that he and Mama left us. But I see now that the memories of them that I chose to look at again and again, were only snapshot moments in time. Like the photo Daddy left on the pillow, more was happening than is apparent on the glossy surface, behind the smiles, beyond the borders. Another shot might've shown my mother looking away from the camera to some distant place, my father watching her with a longing so intense, it bordered on sickness. Still another might've shown another facet of them both, of all of us.

I close my eyes and see his young face smiling down at me with such love and promise as he twirled me around in his arms in the yard, then again as I danced on top of his feet. The scene in my mind shifts, and I see his stricken face as he looked at Dottie and me one last time before leaving us at Aunt Maeve's when we were little.

He loved us. He intended to come back on that day he drove away from the trailer, the day he left to find

Mama and bring her home. *But even with the best intentions sometimes things don't work out like you plan.*

I open my eyes. As I watch him climb into the cab and close the door, watch it pull away, I whisper the words I couldn't say to him back then because my throat was too thick with fear. Because I wanted to believe his promise that he'd be back again, quick as a whistle.

"Goodbye, Daddy." *I've found the good memories I lost. That's how I'll remember you from now on.*

"You were right," Dottie says. "He and Mama… they didn't hold on tight enough."

"I don't think they knew how."

Her sigh is sad.

But I don't have any room left for sadness. Today, my home was full. And so is my heart. Soon there'll be a baby in my life. A nephew. That's a first. A sweet surprise that I never expected. A new member of the family that I realize now means everything to me. Not the perfect storybook family I imagined having one day.

But, as Dottie would say, perfect's not all it's cracked up to be. I will welcome my nephew into my perfectly imperfect life—my family—with open arms.

And hold on tight.

You're never too old to sneak out at night

BJ thinks her younger sister, Iris, needs a love interest. So she does what any mature woman would do and organizes an Over-Fifty Singles Night. When her matchmaking backfires it turns out to be the best thing either of them could have hoped for.

Over 50's Singles Night

by Ellyn Bache

HN37

Available April 2006
TheNextNovel.com

There are things inside us
we don't know how to express,
but that doesn't mean
they're not there.

A poignant story about a woman
coming to terms with her relationship
with her father and learning to open up
to the other men in her life.

The Birdman's Daughter

by Cindi Myers

Available April 2006
TheNextNovel.com

HN38

REQUEST YOUR FREE BOOKS!

2 FREE NOVELS TO INTRODUCE YOU TO OUR BRAND-NEW LINE!

There's the life you planned. And there's what comes next.

A forty-something blushing bride?

Neely Mason never expected to walk down the aisle, but it's happening, and now her whole Southern family is in on the event. Can they all get through this wedding without killing each other? Because one thing's for sure, when it comes to sisters, *crazy* is a relative term.

The
GOOD KIND
OF CRAZY

TANYA MICHAELS

A Boca Babe on a Harley?

Harriet's former life as a Boca Babe—where only looks, money and a husband count—left her struggling for freedom. Finally gaining control of her path, she's leaving that life behind as she takes off on her Harley. When she drives straight into a mystery that is connected to her past, will she be able to stay true to her future?

Dirty Harriet

by Miriam Auerbach

HN40

Available April 2006
TheNextNovel.com